LAKE VILLA DISTRICT LIBRARY
(847)356-7711 www.lvdl.org

3 1981 00656 2940

STRONG, HEALTHY GIRLS

HEALTHY ROMANTIC RELATIONSHIPS

By Alexis Burling

CONTENT CONSULTANT
Dr. Amanda J. Rose
Professor of Psychological Sciences
University of Missouri

Essential Library

An Imprint of Abdo Publishing | abdobooks.com

LAKE VILLA DISTRICT LIBRARY
847.356.7711 www.lvdl.org

abdobooks.com

Published by Abdo Publishing, a division of ABDO, PO Box 398166, Minneapolis, Minnesota 55439. Copyright © 2021 by Abdo Consulting Group, Inc. International copyrights reserved in all countries. No part of this book may be reproduced in any form without written permission from the publisher. Essential Library™ is a trademark and logo of Abdo Publishing.

Printed in the United States of America, North Mankato, Minnesota.
082020
012021

THIS BOOK CONTAINS RECYCLED MATERIALS

Cover Photo: Luis Molinero/Shutterstock Images
Interior Photos: Dusan Petkovic/Shutterstock Images, 8; iStockphoto, 10, 13, 16, 25, 34–35, 47, 49, 50, 53, 69, 73, 78, 90; Antonio Diaz/Shutterstock Images, 15; Dragon Images/iStockphoto, 20; SDI Productions/iStockphoto, 23, 39; Sol Stock/iStockphoto, 27, 92; RG Studio/iStockphoto, 28; Iryna Inshyna/Shutterstock Images, 32; Viktor Gladkov/iStockphoto, 37; Lara Belova/iStockphoto, 40; Jacob Lund/iStockphoto, 44; Shutterstock Images, 56, 98–99; Pollyana Ventura/iStockphoto, 58; Prostock Studio/iStockphoto, 61, 97; Juan Monino/iStockphoto, 66; Estrada Anton/Shutterstock Images, 71; People Images/iStockphoto, 74; Wunder Visuals/iStockphoto, 80; StoryTime Studio/Shutterstock Images, 83; Viktor Cvetkovic/iStockphoto, 86–87; Monkey Business Images/Shutterstock Images, 94

Editor: Aubrey Zalewski
Series Designer: Nikki Nordby

Library of Congress Control Number: 2019954397
Publisher's Cataloging-in-Publication Data

Names: Burling, Alexis, author.
Title: Healthy romantic relationships / by Alexis Burling
Description: Minneapolis, Minnesota : Abdo Publishing, 2021 | Series: Strong, healthy girls | Includes online resources and index.
Identifiers: ISBN 9781532192203 (lib. bdg.) | ISBN 9781098210106 (ebook)
Subjects: LCSH: Love in adolescence--Juvenile literature. | Emotions in adolescence--Juvenile literature. | Social psychology--Juvenile literature. | Interpersonal relations--Juvenile literature. | Dating--Juvenile literature.
Classification: DDC 155.533--dc23

CONTENTS

MEET
DR. AMANDA 4

TAKE IT
FROM ME 6

CHAPTER ONE
WHAT'S IN
A CRUSH? 8

CHAPTER TWO
KEEPING YOUR
OPTIONS OPEN 20

CHAPTER THREE
DEFINING YOUR
RELATIONSHIP 32

CHAPTER FOUR
CHOOSING
SAFE SEX 44

CHAPTER FIVE
FIGHTING IS
HEALTHY! 56

CHAPTER SIX
ABUSIVE
RELATIONSHIPS 66

CHAPTER SEVEN
IS IT TIME
TO BREAK UP? 78

CHAPTER EIGHT
COMMITMENT
101 90

A SECOND LOOK 102
PAY IT FORWARD 104
GLOSSARY 106
ADDITIONAL RESOURCES 108
INDEX 110
ABOUT THE AUTHOR 112

DR. AMANDA

Dr. Amanda J. Rose has always been interested in relationships. Our closest relationships can bring us incredible happiness, but when our relationships don't go well, life can be very hard. Different relationships are important at different stages of life, with friendships being especially important for adolescents. Dr. Amanda has been studying girls' friendships for more than 20 years, with more than 5,000 youth participating in her research projects.

    Dr. Amanda grew up in Ohio and went to college at the Ohio State University, where she majored in psychology and minored in English. Her senior thesis was her first research project on adolescence. After graduating summa cum laude, Dr. Amanda went on to study developmental psychology at the University of Illinois at Urbana-Champaign. There she earned her master's degree and her doctorate. For her master's thesis and doctoral dissertation, she studied how girls and boys handle conflict in their friendships and how they support each other in times of stress.

In 1999, Dr. Amanda joined the faculty at the University of Missouri as a founding member of the Developmental Psychology Training Program in the Department of Psychological Sciences. Together with her students, she has conducted many research studies, with a focus on the benefits and challenges of girls' friendships. This research has been funded by the National Institute of Mental Health. During her time at the University of Missouri, Dr. Amanda has received many honors and awards, including an Early Scientific Achievement Award from the Society for Research in Child Development and a Kemper Fellowship for Excellence in Teaching, one of the highest teaching honors awarded at the University of Missouri.

Dr. Amanda lives in Columbia, Missouri, with her husband, her teenage daughter and son, and her yellow Labrador retriever, Charlie.

TAKE IT
FROM ME

Are you ready to be in love? Of course you are. You're smart. You're beautiful. You're interesting and incredibly capable. Who *wouldn't* want to fall in love with you? While having crushes might often seem like a breeze, entering into a romantic situation can be surprisingly complicated. Nurturing it enough so that it blossoms into a healthy, long-lasting relationship might feel impossible.

But don't worry. I've got you covered. In this book, we'll address everything you might want to know, from what it feels like to have a crush to what to do if you're falling in love with your best friend. What's more, we'll dig into the trickiest (and maybe even the most embarrassing) zone. Yes, I'm talking about sex. Thinking about when and when not to have it is a must. Why? Because waiting until the right time is the best decision you'll ever make, whether it's your first time or anytime.

Beyond the physical, we'll also explore the flip side of love: pain. In every romantic relationship, it's important to know how to deal with conflict respectfully and responsibly so that each of you feels heard. As my parents always used to tell me, learning how to pick your battles and knowing when to compromise is the key to any successful partnership.

Finally, we'll tackle the hardest topics, like what to do if your partner is controlling or, worse yet, abusive. I'll also walk you through how to go through a breakup in the healthiest way possible.

I've had my fair share of practice when it comes to romantic relationships. Some of my decisions were excellent and impacted my life in positive ways. But I also made many, *many* mistakes—some humiliating, some hilarious—and lived to tell about them.

Being in love is a tumultuous but amazing ride. Sure, there might be times when it feels like the whole thing isn't worth it. But trust me, it is. Each and every part of the journey is meaningful—the glorious, the devastating, and everything in between.

XOXO,
ALEXIS

CHAPTER ONE

WHAT'S IN A CRUSH?

During middle school, you may have noticed a change in the way you saw your classmates. Maybe you found yourself looking at a boy in your math class and then blushing deeply when he caught you in the act. While that does seem incredibly mortifying, there is a perfectly good reason for your goofy behavior. It's called having a crush—and it's totally normal.

Crushes, or strong feelings of attraction toward another girl or boy can happen at any age after you've hit puberty. Sometimes you are attracted to someone because of a physical quality, such as the way that person looks, dresses, or even smells. In other situations, you might like an aspect of a person's personality, such as a sense of humor or a sweet, compassionate side. In rare instances, you might not even know why you're into someone. But if you start sweating or giggling uncontrollably every time that person is around, chances are high that it's because you have a crush.

So how do you tell the difference between liking a friend or a person in your class a whole lot and having a bona fide crush? Even more unsettling, what do you do with all those feelings once you know you have them? Do you tell the object of your affection

or let it go? Pennie and Justin found themselves deep in the throes of a crush situation with no idea how to handle it.

PENNIE'S STORY

Pennie and Justin had known each other for what seemed like forever. In kindergarten, Justin's family moved to Washington from Minnesota. He didn't know anyone at his new school and was kind of an introvert. Luckily, his parents befriended the family next door, who had a daughter exactly his age. Her name was Pennie.

Pennie and Justin soon became inseparable. Throughout their childhood, they loved climbing trees, building forts, and playing in the mud. When they got older, Pennie made Justin a friendship bracelet out of her mom's beads and yarn. Justin taught Pennie how to fish. They spent long days wading in the river that ran behind both of their houses. Then they would talk about every thought and feeling that popped into their heads while lying next to each other in the grass.

Everything seemed carefree, simple, and easy. But in ninth grade, their friendship shifted. Pennie auditioned for the fall musical and started spending more time with the cast. Justin joined a band and grew out his hair. At least two of Pennie's friends talked about how cute Justin was, but all Pennie could think was, *Wait, my neighbor Justin? I mean, sure, he has decent blue eyes, and he's a great listener, but . . . cute? Really?*

***

One fall day in September, Pennie and her friends were sitting in the cafeteria courtyard obsessing over the homecoming dance. Janet was already going with Michael, the boy she had just started dating. But the rest of them hadn't gotten dates yet. Frannie and Lizette were both gushing over Justin.

"He is just *so* good-looking," Frannie said. "Every time I see him, I think my heart is about to pound right out of my chest."

Pennie stayed quiet as the girls rambled on. Then Lizette said something that caught Pennie's attention. "Well, I'd give three months' allowance to go to the dance with him, but that won't ever happen. He's obviously interested in someone else."

"Who?" Pennie asked.

"Um, hello? Are you blind?" Lizette responded.

TALK ABOUT IT

- **What qualities do you look for in a close friend? Are those the same qualities you find in people you have a crush on, or are they different? Why?**
- **What are some things that can affect a close friendship?**

> "Well, I'd give three months' allowance to go to the dance with him, but that won't ever happen."

Pennie was about to press further. But before she could, Justin and his bandmates walked into the courtyard and sat down next to the girls. Frannie pounced on the opportunity. "So, do you guys have any dates in mind for the homecoming dance?" she asked the group.

"Well, I don't yet, but Justin's clearly going to ask his *girlfriend*," Nigel said with a smug smirk, staring directly at Pennie. Justin immediately turned bright red and looked away, his hair falling over his eyes. Suddenly, Pennie felt incredibly confused. Was Nigel referring to her? Did Justin really think of her that way? Even weirder, did she think about Justin that way?

***

After that day in the courtyard, things became awkward between Pennie and Justin. They certainly didn't talk every day after school as they used to. When Justin saw Pennie in the hall, he'd either turn around and walk the other way or pretend to be looking at his phone when he passed her. Pennie also felt a strange nervous energy anytime she was in the same room with Justin. Even her parents asked her why they hadn't seen Justin around the house as often. Pennie told them he had been really busy writing music and didn't have as much time on his hands.

> **TALK ABOUT IT**
>
> ▪ Have you ever had a crush on a friend? How did you feel when you were with him or her?
> ▪ What do you think is the difference between liking and loving someone?

Two weeks before the homecoming dance, Pennie still didn't have a date. Lizette and Nigel were going together. Frannie and a bunch of other girls had decided to go stag and have fun on their own. As for Justin, Pennie wasn't sure whether he was even going at all. If anything, he'd probably ask Jackie, the supercool bassist in their band and the one every musician in their grade seemed to have a thing for. As time wore on, Pennie decided she'd go with Frannie and her group so she could finally stop thinking about it.

Then, on Friday, a week before homecoming, Pennie saw Justin standing at her locker. She thought about turning around and slinking away, but he caught her eye and waved her over. Pennie felt exhausted from overthinking everything. But she just wanted to know whether Justin was going to the dance. Then she

could stop thinking about it and get over whatever this weirdness was between them. After saying hello, she decided to just ask Justin whether he was going to the dance, suddenly realizing that she'd be bummed if he had decided to skip it altogether.

"So, did you end up asking Jackie?" Pennie asked Justin, her heart beating loudly in her chest. She wanted him to go to the dance, but now a part of her hoped he would say no.

Before Justin could respond, Pennie nervously rambled.

"I like you, and I've liked you for a long time."

"Because I really think you should ask her. You guys would make such a great couple," she said. In her head she knew that Justin and Jackie would be great together. If he hadn't asked Jackie yet, he definitely was going to. Who else would he ask? *Not me*, she thought. *Right?* She continued to pester Justin about asking Jackie for a couple more minutes, barely giving him a chance to talk. Finally, he interrupted her.

TALK ABOUT IT

= **Do you think risking a friendship to pursue a crush is worth it? Why or why not?**

= **Why do you think Pennie suggested that Justin go to the dance with Jackie?**

= **What do you think Pennie is going to do next? Do you think Pennie and Justin should go to the dance together? Why or why not?**

= **What if Pennie didn't like Justin back? How would you handle that situation if you were Pennie?**

"Ugh, cut it out, Pennie. I'm not going to ask Jackie," Justin blurted out.

Pennie stared at him. "I'm not going to ask Jackie because I want to ask you. OK? I like you, and I've liked you for a long time," he said. His face turned beet red once more.

Pennie was suddenly speechless. When she didn't respond right away, Justin brushed the hair out of his eyes, turned around, and hurried down the hall. Pennie watched him go. *Oh*, she thought.

ASK THE EXPERT

Our ability to experience emotions that extend beyond friendship and family relationships begins in adolescence. Unlike kids in elementary school, teens are able to feel infatuation, passion, and even romantic love. Developing these types of feelings and sexual attraction toward others is a natural part of growing up. Having a crush on someone has the power to affect your body and mind without your consent. Understanding these new feelings is anything but simple. Acting on them by asking someone out can be even more complex, especially when it involves someone who is a good friend.

If you're dealing with a crush, there are a number of helpful questions you can ask yourself to get your feelings and thoughts in order. What makes this person so special? How do you feel when you are around your crush? Do you want to act on those feelings? What will you do if your crush doesn't like you back?

If it helps, write down your answers in a journal. You can also talk to a trusted friend, sibling, or adult and hash out these questions together. Your talking buddy can act as your sounding board and hopefully give you solid advice. Dealing with a crush can seem downright impossible. But having a crush can be a fun and exciting time. It's a time to figure out which characteristics attract you. Enjoy it!

GET HEALTHY

- If you have a crush on your friend, decide whether it's worth risking the friendship.
- If your crush makes you feel bad about yourself or treats you poorly, it's time to find a new crush.
- If someone has a crush on you, be sensitive to that person's feelings.
- When telling your crush how you feel, avoid the word *love*. This could put a lot of pressure on you both, making the situation uncomfortable.
- If your crush doesn't feel the same way you do, try not to take it too personally.

THE LAST WORD FROM ALEXIS

What does it feel like to have a crush? For me, it's like my world is covered in yellow daffodils and I've just been gifted a lifetime supply of dark chocolate. Amazing! On the flip side, I then second-guess everything I say and giggle nervously whenever my crush is around. Not cool. But if your experience is anything like mine, the object of your affection probably won't notice your awkward behavior or will find it endearing. Crushing on someone should make you feel giddy, nervous, and hopeful all at the same time. Explore your feelings. Get to know your crush to see whether your impressions of that person are accurate. And one last thing. If it doesn't work out, try not to think of it as a failure. Maybe the timing was off, or maybe you just weren't meant to be together. Either way, take some time to wallow. Then get back out there, girl. You can do this!

CHAPTER TWO

KEEPING YOUR OPTIONS OPEN

It seems as though every time you turn on the television or go see a movie, at least one main character is either thinking about or downright obsessing over dating someone else. Whether you call this going out, hanging out, seeing someone, or even talking to someone, dating is usually a nerve-racking, thrilling, and all-consuming experience. But what does dating actually mean? How does a person go from having a crush to being involved?

For teens and even adults, dating can mean a number of different things. Some people equate dating to being in a serious, monogamous relationship. Others consider dating to be the step that happens before you decide whether you want to be exclusive. It's spending time with someone to get to know him or her better before committing to each other.

Whichever way you see it, there are a few general guidelines you can follow to keep your dating experiences healthy and positive. First, think carefully about how you choose to date, but try not to overthink it to the point that you're causing yourself excess stress. Next, if you're not sure whom you want to date, keep your options open before taking the plunge. Get to know a few different people casually before you decide to enter into a relationship. If you go this route, remember to communicate clearly and be up-front with everyone about your intentions as much as possible. Finally, always treat people with respect. Read on to see how Sadie handles—and sometimes fumbles in—the dating world.

> Get to know a few different people casually before you decide to enter into a relationship.

SADIE'S STORY

Sadie was one of those girls who seemed like she could do it all without breaking a sweat. She was the smartest girl in her junior class and was the cocaptain of the swim team. Many of the guys in her grade—and even some seniors—had a crush on her. Most of the girls thought she was great too. Because Sadie made a point of being nice and, more importantly, genuine to everyone no matter which clique they were in, she had a lot of fans.

Being so popular made Sadie's social life seem like a breeze. But what many of her friends didn't realize was that Sadie felt unsure and insecure a lot of the time. For her, making friends

was easy. But dating—and more specifically figuring out *whom* to date and what counted as a date—was what caused all the trouble.

Take Sadie's friend Austin, for example. He was well liked, got good grades, and threw excellent parties. Lately, Sadie and Austin had started spending more time together along with a bunch of their friends. The weekend prior, they had gone to their first movie alone. Austin even bought the tickets and a popcorn for them to share. When Sadie told her friends about their outing, they all insisted it must have been a date. But was it, even though nothing (like kissing) had happened? And if Austin thought it was, did she want it to be?

TALK ABOUT IT

- **What makes something a date? How is it different from doing something alone with a friend?**
- **If you were Sadie, would you have considered your outing with Austin to be a date? Why or why not?**

***

In addition to the Austin issue, something else had recently popped up in Sadie's life—or, more specifically, some*one*. Her name was Becky. She was Sadie's cocaptain on the swim team. Aside from being a stellar diver with a whiz-bang sense of humor, Becky was also one of the few girls at school who was openly gay. Because of her confidence, winning personality, and go-getter attitude, most people accepted Becky for who she was.

One day after swim practice, Becky offered Sadie a ride home. But instead of dropping her off right away, the girls decided to stop by the local pizza joint for a quick slice. What started off as a one-hour outing turned into a three-hour excursion—the most time they'd ever spent together solo. In fact, Sadie didn't realize it had gotten so late until her dad sent her a text asking whether she'd be home for dinner.

"You know, we should totally do this more often," Becky said as they got in the car. "I mean, I know we rock the swim team together, but I had no idea you were so awesome. What about a weekly thing?" Sadie smiled.

"Hey, thanks! Um, yeah, that'd be fun! My brother usually needs the car, so I'm sure he'd appreciate my getting a ride too," Sadie said.

"Well, never mind your brother," Becky said with a grin as she pulled up to Sadie's house. "I'm asking because I definitely want to hang with you more often."

***

TALK ABOUT IT

- What do you notice about Becky's behavior? How is it different from Sadie's?
- Have you ever been up-front about telling someone how you feel about them? If so, how did you tell them? How did it work out?

That night, Sadie couldn't stop thinking about what Becky had said. When she pictured Becky's face, she felt a warm tingling in her chest that hadn't been there before. What was going on?

For the next few weeks, Sadie felt confused. Though she hadn't hung out with Austin again since that time at the movies, he continued to stop by before swim practice and text her all the time. Sadie was pretty sure she wasn't into Austin as more than a friend, but she didn't know how to tell him. When he asked her to make plans, she kept making excuses. She also stopped responding to most of his texts.

Meanwhile, every time she hung out with Becky, that same tingly feeling emerged. Sure, they talked about their latest fashion finds. But they also discussed deeper stuff, like their family life

> She just wasn't sure about any of the feelings she was having lately.

and what they wanted to do after high school. Becky even asked Sadie whether she had any crushes, but Sadie never had a clear answer. She just wasn't sure about any of the feelings she was having lately.

Then one night everything came to a head. Austin sent Sadie a blunt text, asking why she was ignoring him and saying he would stop "bothering" her from now on. When Sadie told Becky about it the next day, Becky looked at her with an understanding smile.

"Well, I'm not exactly surprised. He clearly liked you and you kind of sent him mixed messages," Becky said. "You should talk to him and explain your side of the story. And listen. Hopefully this doesn't freak you out, but I think you're pretty cool and would like whatever this is to keep going. And I'm not sure, but it seems like you might think I'm pretty cool too. Either way, I want to see where this goes."

Sadie smiled, totally forgetting about Austin. She still wasn't sure about her feelings. But she really liked the way things were going so far with Becky. She replied, "Yeah, me too."

TALK ABOUT IT

- How do you think Sadie handled the situation with Austin? If you were in her shoes, how would you have handled it?
- What are some reasons why hanging out with a few people before committing to a serious relationship could be a good thing? Why might it be bad?
- What are some things you can do when you aren't sure about your feelings?

ASK THE EXPERT

When you're young, it's tempting to rush into a relationship before you're ready. Because life feels so visceral all the time, it's easy to go from "Will you go to the movies with me?" to "I love you forever" in the span of a week. But sometimes *not* jumping on the romance train too quickly is a good first step in discovering what you want, whom you like, and why you might like a person.

One of the most important things to remember before you're starting to date—and even after you've become more experienced and had a few long-term relationships—is that nothing is set in stone. Just because you've gone out with someone once, or even a few times, doesn't mean you must continue doing so. If you two aren't aligned for whatever reason—personality, life outlook, hobbies, desires—it's fine to just call it a day and continue on as friends or acquaintances.

On the other hand, if you decide you do like someone more than as a friend and want to get to know him or her better, it's best to communicate that intention clearly, as Becky did. This avoids mix-ups, like what happened with Sadie and Austin. Again, take things slow until you feel you're ready. Though it may feel like a snail's pace, it'll save you from heartache in the end.

GET **HEALTHY**

- Try hanging out with different types of people as friends before you get serious with one person. It'll help you figure out whom you want to be with and why.
- If you're not sure whether you like girls or boys, why not try them both out as an option?
- Exploring your options is great but not if it's behind someone's back. Whether you're hanging out as friends or trying out dating, make sure each person is on the same page about where the relationship stands. Not doing so could cause major problems and hurt others' feelings.
- Don't feel like you have to rush into anything. Take as much time as you need.

THE LAST WORD FROM **ALEXIS**

I know what some of you might be thinking: how is Sadie contemplating dating two people when you can't even find one to date? I get it. Truth be told, I only dated one person during my years in high school. Still, keeping your options open before committing to one person is not only simpler but smarter. That way you can really take a deep dive when getting to know your prospective partners—their interests, their talents, and their annoying habits—before you decide to become officially involved. Then, when it's finally time to make your relationship a reality, you can focus on the good stuff.

CHAPTER THREE

DEFINING YOUR RELATIONSHIP

In many cases, casually hanging out with a potential romantic partner can feel like a stroll in the park. You go see movies or attend concerts on Friday nights with this boy or girl you sort of know. You flirt a bit and message each other before bed. Maybe you go to school dances and hang at the beach on weekends with some of your other pals in tandem. It feels totally blissful, carefree, adventurous, and fun.

But full-on commitment? That's another story. When you're in a monogamous relationship with someone, you're dating only that person—and no one else. You're in it for the long haul until you decide to break up. While that can seem totally suffocating for some ill-matched couples, it can also be truly wonderful and life-changing for others, especially if you're with someone you care about.

Like many situations having to do with love and romance, it can be bewildering to know how to define your relationship and when to make it official. What do you say? When do you say it? If you've been hanging out casually for a while, what if the person decides he or she doesn't like you back, or worse, laughs in your face when you say you might want something more from the relationship? While that latter part probably won't happen (and if it does, your supposed partner needs a compassion check), there are a few things you can do to make the process go more smoothly.

> It can be bewildering to know how to define your relationship and when to make it official.

When Aliyah's feelings for Layla grew, Aliyah had to figure out how to go from good friends to girlfriends.

ALIYAH'S STORY

Aliyah and Layla met each other at summer camp in New Hampshire when they were in eighth grade. Now they went to the same high school and had been hanging out casually for three months. In the past, Aliyah had dated other girls. But the periodic

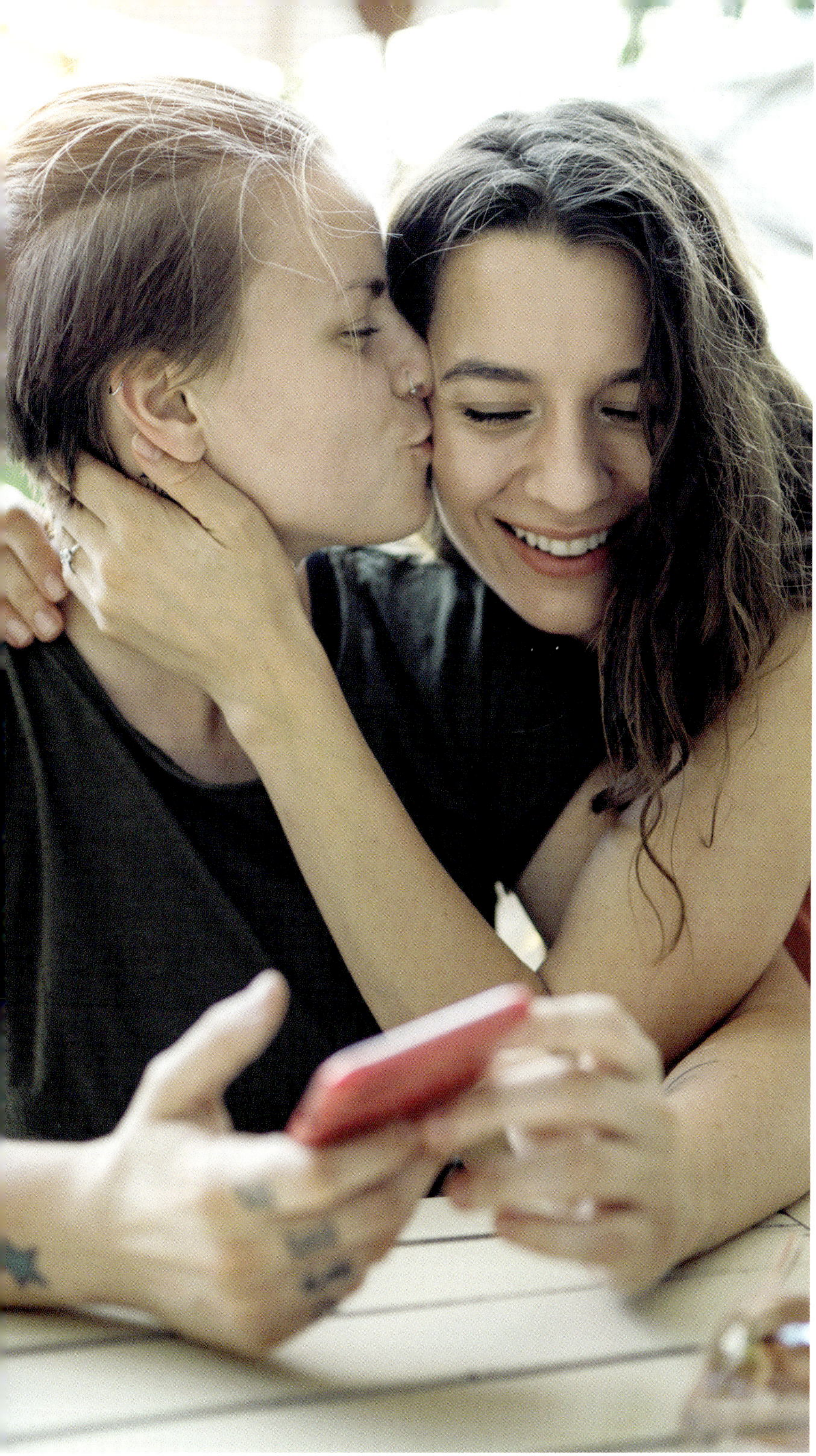

dinners at Aliyah's house and picnics in the park were Layla's first experience with anything close to being romantic.

When they first started hanging out, Aliyah thought about other girls even when she was with Layla. When they went out shopping or got together to study for a geometry exam, Aliyah would sometimes text Danika or Agnes just to see what they were doing. It wasn't that Aliyah wasn't into Layla. But she wasn't *super* into Layla either.

Then, right around the three-month mark, Aliyah noticed a change in the way she felt about Layla. Sometimes she found herself staring at Layla, thinking about how pretty and kind she was. Other times, when she was by herself and desperately in need of advice, she'd often wonder what Layla might do in the situation.

TALK ABOUT IT

- **Is it OK that Aliyah thought about other people while she was hanging out with Layla? Why or why not?**
- **Have you ever started hanging out with someone casually but then noticed a change in your feelings? Were there signs? If so, what were some of them?**

Consequently, she stopped responding to other girls' texts and requests to hang out. Whether she wanted to admit it to herself or not, these days all Aliyah wanted to do was be around Layla.

***

One Saturday night, when the girls were at their usual hangout spot by the lake, Layla brought up something Aliyah had been thinking about for quite some time but was too scared to mention. "So, um, I was wondering," she said, tentatively. "Are you still hanging out with Danika?"

Aliyah felt her heart skip a beat. She wasn't quite sure how to respond. Should she come clean about what had been on her mind the last few weeks?

"Oh, Danika? Um, not really so much anymore," Aliyah said. "I mean, I think she's cool, but we don't have that much in common. Plus, I've had other things on my mind lately and have wanted to sort that out."

Layla's breath caught in her throat. "So, are you hanging out with anyone else, then? I mean, besides me?" she asked Aliyah in a soft voice.

Aliyah paused, then coughed. "It's freezing out here! Leave it to us to have a picnic in the cold," she said, laughing awkwardly. "But, um . . . No. I'm not hanging out with anyone else really. I've just been so busy lately. Why?"

TALK ABOUT IT

- **Why do you think Aliyah didn't reveal her feelings for Layla at their picnic?**
- **Why do you think Layla didn't explain the real reason she asked Aliyah whether she was still seeing Danika?**
- **Have you ever been scared about having a conversation that might define your relationship with someone? What are some of your fears surrounding that situation?**

Layla looked away, clearly anxious as well but trying not to show it. "Oh, well, no reason, I guess," she said after a minute. "I was just curious."

***

The next day at school, Layla acted a bit more standoffish than usual. Instead of sitting with Aliyah at lunch, she went to the library to draw. In geometry, they got their test results back, and Layla got an A, but she didn't seem happy even though geometry was her toughest subject. Aliyah noticed something was wrong and tried to cheer Layla up, but even her corny jokes didn't seem to work.

> Layla looked away, clearly anxious as well but trying not to show it.

Aliyah had a strong hunch about why Layla was upset. Aliyah had been through this phase before in a potential relationship and still found it difficult to navigate. In the past, she hadn't been direct enough about wanting more, and things had ended in heartache. This time, she hoped for a different outcome. Before giving herself a chance to chicken out, she messaged Layla to meet her outside the auditorium after school.

When Layla arrived, Aliyah could tell she was nervous. Trying not to make matters worse, she jumped right in. "So, I noticed you seemed a little bummed out today," Aliyah told Layla.

"I'm just a little tired," Layla replied.

There was a pause of awkward silence. Aliyah gathered her courage to say what had been on her mind for a while. "So about yesterday," she began, "I wasn't exactly up-front during our conversation. The real reason I haven't been hanging out with Danika isn't because I've been busy. I mean, yeah, that's true. But it's more that I'd rather be with you. I guess I haven't really known what to say and how to tell you that, but I kind of would love it if you'd be my girlfriend."

Both girls blushed deep crimson. "Well, yeah," Layla replied with a grin. "I'd like that."

TALK ABOUT IT

- Have you ever asked someone to be your girlfriend or boyfriend? If so, how did it go?
- At the end of the story, Aliyah reveals her feelings for Layla. Do you think she did a good job? Is there anything you would do differently?
- Why might it be important to define a relationship and share your feelings with someone you're interested in?

ASK THE EXPERT

Defining a potential romantic relationship and whether you want to take it to a more serious, exclusive level is no easy matter. First, you have to figure out whether you're ready. Then you have to find the best words to express what you really mean and share them in a way your potential partner will understand. Finally, it's all about timing. Pinning down the right moment to have the conversation so it doesn't happen too early or too late is key.

Though it might feel scary, it's important to talk openly about your intentions and feelings when defining a relationship. It helps both people figure out where they stand and whether they want the same thing. Sure, everyone wants to avoid being rejected. But not communicating clearly because you're afraid your feelings might not be reciprocated is just keeping you stuck in limbo longer than you need to be.

Asking someone what he or she wants out of a relationship is a great way to start the "define the relationship" talk. Saying what you want first is even more powerful. Not only does it prevent confusion but it also gives you a chance to demonstrate your confidence in your connection. If your potential partner doesn't feel the same way or isn't ready to make a commitment and wants to keep things casual, try not to let it get you down.

You don't want to move forward in a relationship if you both want different things or are heading in different directions.

GET HEALTHY

- Before having a "define the relationship" talk, think about what being exclusive means and whether you're ready for that kind of commitment.
- Pick a private place you can talk. Be clear about how you feel and listen to the other person's response without interrupting.
- Think of defining a relationship as more than one talk. Sometimes it takes a few times to get it right!
- If your potential partner isn't ready for commitment yet, try not to take it personally.
- Be flexible about the outcome. The fewer expectations you have and the more open-minded you are, the better off you'll be.

THE LAST WORD FROM ALEXIS

Being head over heels in love is one of the best feelings in the entire world! But, at the risk of being obvious, there's that one giant step that needs to happen before you become a couple: making sure you both want the same thing. Believe me, I know putting yourself out there is awkward. Being vulnerable and expressing your desires can feel super embarrassing. So here's a little activity you can do to help you. If you're about to have the "define the relationship" talk, do whatever it takes to feel like the Wonder Woman you are. Maybe that means going for a run first or putting on your favorite song and singing your brains out in the shower to boost your self-confidence. Then, once you're feeling confident, take the plunge. I'm rooting for you!

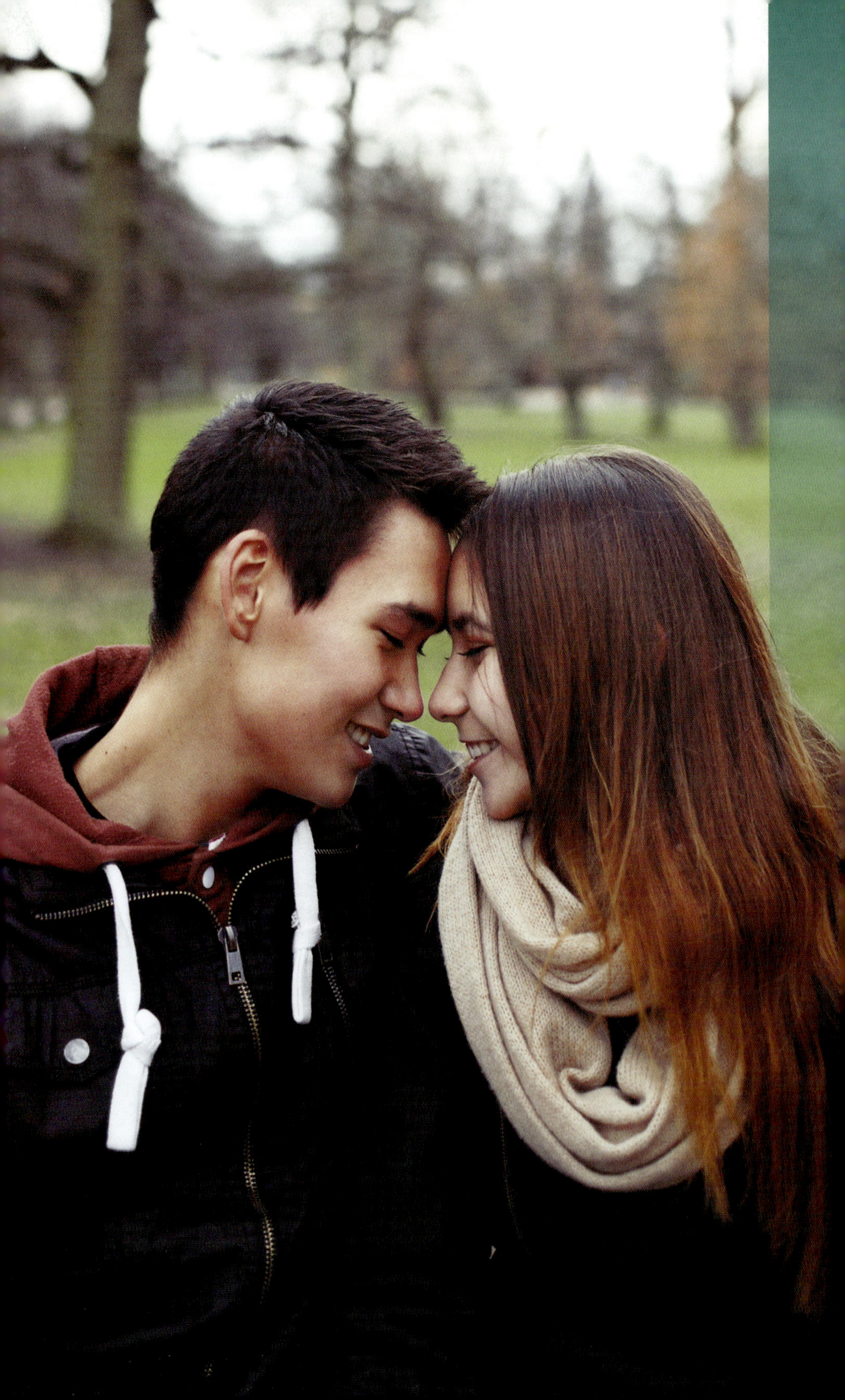

CHAPTER FOUR

CHOOSING SAFE SEX

Being physically intimate with a partner is like no other feeling in the world. But whether or not we want to acknowledge it, having sex comes with a lot of serious responsibility. It permanently alters your life and your relationship. Just this one act has the power to affect the way you feel about yourself and the way others feel about you.

There are also mental and physical health risks involved. For one thing, being forced to have sex when you're not willing or ready to can cause emotional trauma. Unprotected sex can lead to pregnancy. It can also leave you vulnerable to sexually transmitted infections such as herpes, chlamydia, gonorrhea, hepatitis B, human papillomavirus (HPV), or human immunodeficiency virus (HIV), the virus that causes AIDS.

For these reasons, sex—and every step leading up to it—is not something that should be taken lightly, rushed through, or barely thought about. Sex isn't some goal that you need to check off or brag about to impress your friends. Instead, in an ideal world, sex is a beautiful, intimate act that happens between willing partners who have given each other consent. It should be done in a comfortable environment that allows each participant to feel safe, confident, and loved. Carrie and Alex are in a committed relationship and are considering having sex for the first time. But is Carrie sure that she's ready?

> In an ideal world, sex is a beautiful, intimate act that happens between willing partners who have given each other consent.

CARRIE'S STORY

It was a week before the December holidays, and juniors Carrie and Alex were celebrating their one-year anniversary on Sunday. They planned a romantic date that involved a fancy Greek dinner plus a stroll along the waterfront. Alex's parents were also going to a party that night, so he and Carrie would have some time alone together in the house if they planned it right.

Carrie was pumped about the date. She really loved Alex, and the two were exchanging small presents to mark the occasion.

There was also the possibility that they'd have sex for the first time, which made her excited but incredibly nervous because she was not sure she was ready. What if she messed it up? As per usual, her closest friends, Mindy and Betts, were helping her work through the situation—sort of.

"So, are you psyched for the big night tonight?" Betts asked as they sipped their sodas at the local sandwich shop.

"Yeah, are you wearing something hot? Hopefully Alex's parents won't come home in the middle. Hello, embarrassing!" Mindy said, giggling. "How lucky are you? I can't even nail down a boyfriend, and you're already thinking about losing your virginity."

The truth was that Carrie hadn't thought about what she would wear. Her wardrobe consisted mostly of jeans and T-shirts, so changing into some lacy lingerie and lighting candles was definitely not her thing. Frankly, she and Alex hadn't actually *talked* about having sex. But they had done just about everything else physical. He had hinted about it a few times, so she just assumed tonight was the night it would happen.

"I'll probably just throw on my nicer pair of jeans," Carrie said, laughing it off. "But, hey, who knows? I guess you'll find out first thing tomorrow!"

***

Later that afternoon, Carrie was in her bedroom, listening to music and getting ready. True to form, she decided on a new pair of jeggings and her favorite black sweater with a splash of lip gloss. She sent a quick picture of her outfit to Mindy and Betts, and they both gave her the thumbs-up. Meanwhile, she was trying to relax and feel calm, but she couldn't stop the butterflies from careening around in her stomach. Suddenly, she heard a knock on the door.

"Carrie, can I come in?" It was her father. He popped his head through the door. "I just wanted to pop in to see how you

TALK ABOUT IT

- Are you nervous about having sex? Why or why not?
- If you're in a relationship, do you and your partner talk about having sex? How do you talk about it? Do you feel like you can be open and honest about your feelings?
- Do you think it's important to talk with your partner about having sex? Why or why not?

were doing. I've heard you pacing back and forth for an hour now. Is everything OK? Ooo! You look nice!"

"Um, I'm fine, Dad. Thank you. Just a little anxious about going out with Alex tonight," Carrie said.

"I know we've already talked about this before, and I don't want to embarrass you, but . . ." Carrie's father said, gently.

"Daaaaad! I already know what you're going to say." Back when she and Alex had first started going out, her dad had brought up the topic of birth control. Between that and what she had learned in health class, Carrie felt like she knew everything she needed to know already. "I mean, I appreciate it, but can we not have this talk *again*, especially right now? Super embarrassing," Carrie said, clearly exasperated.

"All right, all right. I just wanted to make sure in case, you know, you wanted to ask me anything," Carrie's dad replied.

"Woah, Dad. Thanks. I, um, appreciate it," Carrie said, giving her dad an awkward hug. "I'm just trying to focus on having a good time tonight. Nothing crazy is going to happen. It's just Alex."

***

On Monday, Carrie and Alex were back at school as usual. They were holding hands in the hall. Alex had snuck a surprise rose into Carrie's locker, which made her smile. Still, her friends noticed that Carrie seemed a little off. As soon as they had a chance to grab her, they whisked her away to the drama club's greenroom, where they could talk in private.

"Tell us everything!" Mindy said, giving Carrie's arm a squeeze. "Did you have sex? Was it great? Were you nervous? How did it feel?"

"Slow down and catch a breath!" Betts said. "Let her speak."

"So, um, yes, I am no longer a virgin," Carrie whispered. The girls let out a collective whoop. "It was fine."

> Carrie felt like she knew everything she needed to know already.

TALK ABOUT IT

- Carrie isn't sure whether she is ready to have sex. How do you know when you're ready?

- Do you think it's important to talk to a parent, guardian, or other adult about sex or birth control? Why or why not?

- What do you know about birth control and using protection during sex?

"Fine? That's all you're going to give us? Fine?" Mindy said. "The least you could do is give us some details."

"Well, the dinner was lovely. He looked great and even wore a tie. And . . . the walk along the waterfront was really romantic. He gave me a necklace with both of our initials," Carrie explained. "We decided to stream a movie afterward, but we didn't really get a chance to watch it because, you know."

"That sounds so perfect!" Betts squealed. Her excitement died when she saw that Carrie had started crying. "Carrie, what's wrong? Are you OK?"

"Yeah, sorry," Carrie said, wiping her eyes. "I feel so stupid. The night was really nice, but I guess maybe I wasn't ready after all? He didn't have a condom, but we had sex anyway. Then today, it's like everything's back to normal. He's being super sweet, but he clearly told his friends. They literally keep patting him on the back. And we haven't really talked about it at all. I mean, what if I'm pregnant?"

Betts and Mindy were silent. They wrapped Carrie in a bear hug.

"Yikes. Well, never mind his friends. But maybe it might be a good idea to talk to Alex," Betts said, trying to reassure Carrie. "It's also probably smart to go to your doctor or the nurse and explain the situation."

Carrie took a deep breath and sighed. "You're right," she said. "Thank you for listening. Can you maybe come with me to see if the nurse is there now?"

"Of course we can," Mindy said.

TALK ABOUT IT

- **Why do you think Carrie feels bad about losing her virginity?**
- **If you were Betts or Mindy, what advice would you give Carrie?**

ASK THE EXPERT

Sex, or any level of physical intimacy, is a huge part of healthy romantic relationships. As Carrie discovered, feeling pressure from your friends, your partner, or even yourself to have sex before you're ready or prepared can have real consequences. Knowing—and sticking to—the ground rules about when and how to have responsible sex is a must at all times.

If you're feeling unsure, there's nothing wrong with choosing to wait. If your partner continues to pressure you or starts acting possessive and mean, it's time to think about whether he or she is the right person for you. If your partner attempts to force you to do something you don't want to do, get out of the situation as swiftly as possible. Then tell a trusted person about what happened so he or she can help you figure out what to do next.

If you decide you're ready to have sex, staying safe during intercourse is *always* important. Irresponsible sex puts your health at risk. It's also possible to get pregnant the first time or any time you have sex without proper birth control. Consistent and correct use of condoms is the most effective way to protect yourself from sexually transmitted infections and pregnancy. Being a strong girl in a healthy romantic relationship means being in control of your body, knowing what you want, expressing yourself clearly about those desires, and always staying safe.

GET **HEALTHY**

- Talk to your doctor or a trusted adult about which birth control option is right for you before you plan to have sex.
- Don't rely on your partner to have condoms on hand. Keep a stash of your own to use just in case.
- Openly communicate with your partner about when to get intimate, how to get intimate, and when you're uncomfortable.
- Understand each other's boundaries. Think about what yours are, independently of your partner's. Then come together to agree on a plan.
- Ask for consent—and give your own—before you begin any act of physical intimacy. No always means no.

THE LAST WORD FROM **ALEXIS**

I hope you understand why it's important to stay safe during intercourse. If you're not having sex yet, don't worry! It'll happen in due time. I'm glad I waited until the perfect guy came around so I could look back on the experience with a smile. And one more thing: if you do have unprotected sex and are worried about being pregnant, you have options. Emergency contraception, such as the morning-after pill, is available either over the counter or through a prescription. But it should only be used as a last resort. It's not an effective form of birth control. Keep in mind that the sooner the pills are taken, the more likely they are to be effective. Talk to a medical professional or a trusted adult for more information.

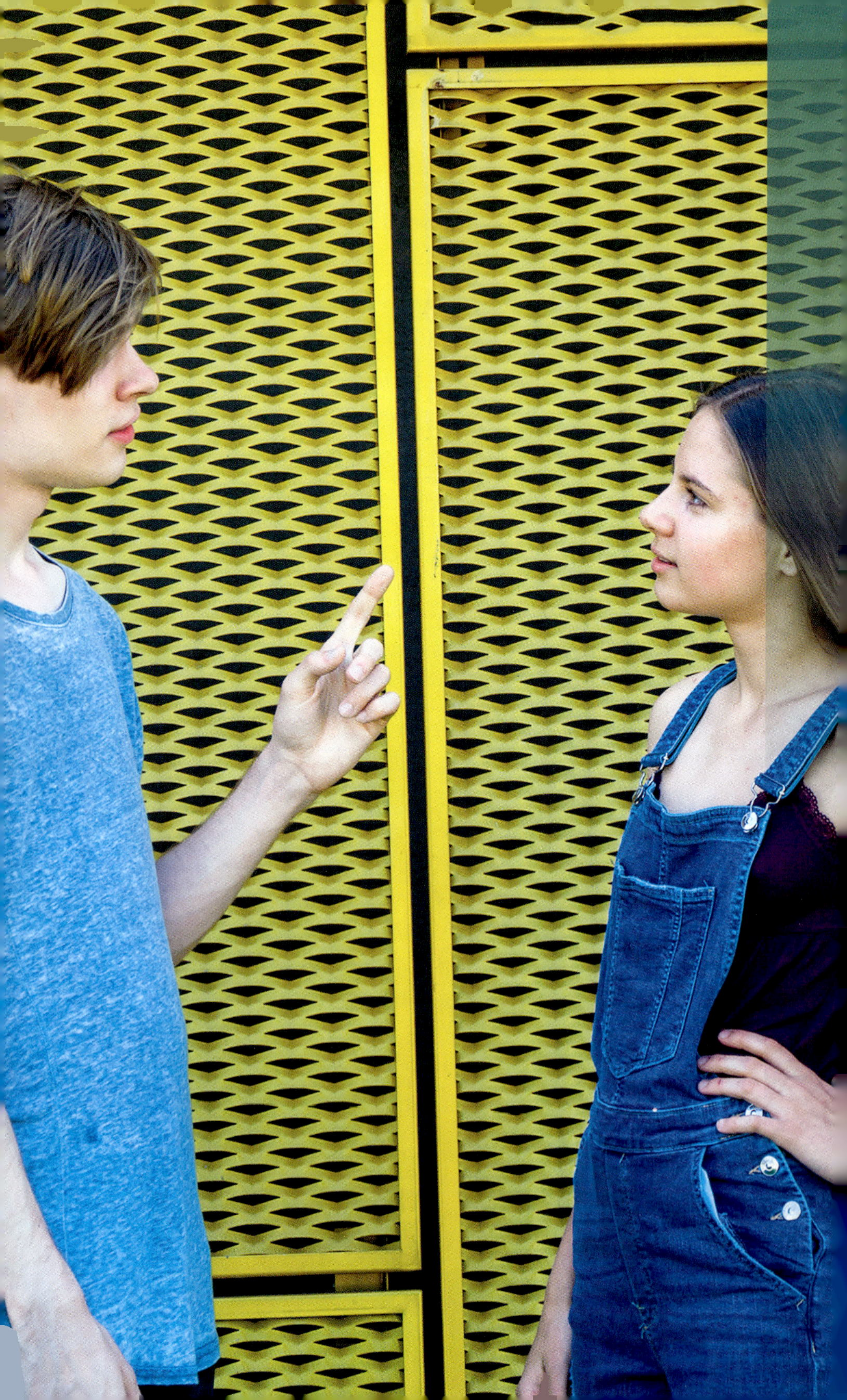

CHAPTER FIVE

FIGHTING IS HEALTHY!

There's no way around it: fighting is the worst. Maybe your parents argue all the time and you're sick of it. Or maybe you're in a relationship and you and your partner can't stop bickering about the little things. Either way, no matter how big or small it is, a fight can often feel like the end of the world.

But here's a news flash: fights are inevitable in any relationship. Why? Because we're all human and it's natural—sometimes even good—to disagree. In fact, according to two studies from 2018 and 2019, couples who argue healthily are more likely to have a happy relationship and stay together than those who ignore problems or pretend they don't exist. Yes, expressing anger to a romantic partner causes discomfort in the short term, but it also sparks honest conversations that can improve a couple's connection over the course of the relationship. What that means is that having constructive conflicts with your partner can actually bring you closer together.

So how do you keep your fights productive and healthy? How do you prevent them from turning into explosive situations full of anger, shame, or passive-aggressive behavior? Read on to learn how Brooke and Jackson succeeded—and stumbled—when navigating an issue affecting their relationship.

BROOKE'S STORY

Every year, Brooke threw a party for her birthday. It fell during the summer vacation, when everyone was off from school, so she usually reserved the outdoor pavilion at the beach near her house. This year was no different. She had invited all her friends, mostly sophomores and juniors but some seniors and freshmen thrown in for good measure.

Brooke's dad had cooked up a few trays of fried chicken for the event. Her boyfriend, Jackson, had made his signature well-curated playlist of Brooke's favorite tunes so everyone could dance. As Brooke looked around at the scene, she saw people she knew everywhere—lounging around on blankets, playing Frisbee, and running back and forth into the waves.

But despite it being her special day, Brooke felt seriously out of sorts this time around— and it definitely had to do with Jackson. Brooke's best friend, Maggie, pulled her aside to ask whether everything was all right.

"It's fine. I'm fine. It's just that Jackson is driving me crazy," Brooke fumed. "Have you

> But despite it being her special day, Brooke felt seriously out of sorts.

seen the way he's been following that new girl around like a puppy dog?"

"Olivia? She's here?" Maggie asked. "That was nice of you to invite her. I'm sure she doesn't really know anyone. Maybe he's just being nice and showing her around."

"Whatever," Brooke muttered. "I only invited her because I felt bad. But now I wish I hadn't. I only met her once, and now Jackson can't stop flirting with her like she's some goddess. He hasn't left her side all night. And it's my party!"

***

Brooke tried to forget about Olivia and enjoy herself. She swam in the ocean with Maggie and some other girls from her dance team. Jackson gave a toast to "the sweetest, most wonderful girlfriend a guy could ask for" before bringing out the cake. Brooke closed her eyes and made a wish, and everyone clapped.

Then it was time to turn up the music and get the party started! When her favorite song came on, Brooke screamed. Everyone gathered around her as she started dancing. It all felt so magical until she looked over and saw Olivia dancing next to Jackson.

> **TALK ABOUT IT**
>
> ▪ **Why do you think Brooke is so fixated on Olivia at the beginning of the story?**
>
> ▪ **If you were Maggie, how would you have responded to Brooke's comments?**

Brooke stormed over to Olivia and stood right in her face. "Why are you dancing with Jackson? Don't you know he's my boyfriend?" Brooke said loudly, causing the people around her to stop dancing and look in their direction.

"Uh. I . . . yes, of course I know he's your boyfriend. He just gave that toast for you," Olivia said, bewildered. "He's been talking about you all night, telling me how amazing you are. I've been wanting to come over to talk to you, but you've been surrounded by your friends. I'm sorry if it looked like something shady was happening. I'm just . . . not really that great at parties when I don't know a lot of people."

> Now she felt stupid for causing such a scene.

Brooke looked at Jackson. He didn't look happy with her at all. Plus, now she felt stupid for causing such a scene. Luckily, Maggie stepped in at that exact moment and announced it was time for a boys-against-girls game of beach volleyball.

***

While the others gathered together on the makeshift volleyball court, Jackson tugged on Brooke's arm, holding her back from the group. "Can we talk for a second?" Jackson asked. "Why did you call out Olivia in front of so many people? She barely knows anyone. It made you look bad."

"*Me* look bad? I'm not the one who was attached to her hip all night," Brooke replied. "I mean, if you want to date other people, you should just say so, Jackson."

"Date other people? What are you talking about? Are you jealous?" Jackson asked.

"Jealous? Of Olivia? No way," Brooke scoffed. But if she was

TALK ABOUT IT

- What do you think of Brooke's behavior?
- If you were Brooke, what would you have done?
- Brooke is clearly upset with Jackson. Why do you think she lashed out at Olivia instead of Jackson?

honest with herself, she was jealous—and hurt. She took a deep breath, then let it out. "Instead of spending the night by my side, my boyfriend was basically hanging out with another girl in front of all our friends. It made me feel bad."

Jackson paused and thought about what Brooke had said. In fact, what she said was true. He had been so busy worrying about whether Olivia felt comfortable around so many strangers that he hadn't stopped to think about whether his girlfriend was having a good time. He felt sheepish. "You're right. I'm so sorry," he said quietly. "I definitely don't want to be in a relationship with anyone else. Olivia's nice and all, but I only have eyes for you."

He leaned over and kissed her on the cheek. "But can I say one more thing?"

"Sure," Brooke said.

"I don't think jealousy is a good thing," Jackson said. "In the future, can we just talk about things that are bothering us?"

Brooke gave him a quick kiss back. "Yeah, let's do that."

TALK ABOUT IT

- **What do you think Brooke learned in her fight with Jackson, if anything? What do you think Jackson learned?**
- **Would you consider this a healthy fight or an unhealthy fight? Why?**
- **When you fight with your partner or friends, are they mostly healthy fights or unhealthy fights? How do you think you could improve?**

ASK THE EXPERT

In this story, Brooke and Jackson have a fight because of one of the most common emotions: jealousy. But instead of addressing the problem head-on in a respectful way, Brooke allowed tension to build until an argument occurred. This type of heated discussion—especially one done in front of other people—doesn't solve anything.

To argue in the healthiest way possible, it's best if emotions—and voices—remain as calm and rational as possible. This allows each person to get out what they want without having to go on the defensive. In other words, name-calling should be avoided at all costs. If you're unhappy with something your partner has done, you shouldn't place blame, either. Try talking about how the action made you feel. Then listen to your partner's response. It could be that they really didn't realize that what they were doing upset you.

Another important point to keep in mind is that most happy couples tend to take a solution-oriented approach to conflict. That means working together to come to a mutually beneficial goal. Sometimes one or both of you might have to compromise or change your behavior even if you don't want to. But remember, the person you are arguing with is your loved one, not your enemy. In relationship disagreements, the goal isn't to win. It's to try to get to a place where both of you feel heard and feel that your needs are met, even if you have different opinions.

GET HEALTHY

- If something is bothering you about your partner's behavior, don't avoid it. Address it head-on.
- If you feel your temper flair during a fight, stop and take a breath before responding. A little rational thinking goes a long way.
- Don't use accusatory, judgmental, or provocative language.
- Remain in the present and stay on topic. Don't bring up things from the past, and try not to exaggerate. Pushing harder than you need to will only incite defensiveness in your partner and make you look like a bully.
- Be willing to compromise.

THE LAST WORD FROM ALEXIS

If you're anything like I am, you love a feisty argument. Give me a challenge, and I can debate it until everyone's tired of hearing my voice—myself included. But fighting until the bitter end isn't always a good idea. In that situation, even when you win, you still lose big time. If you're in a spat with your partner, try to look at it as an opportunity for learning and growth. Let go of the little stuff. If you did something you are ashamed of, own up to your mistake. A sincere apology goes a long way. And finally, try to remind yourself why you like or love your partner, even during the heat of the squabble. Sure, you might still be angry now or even a few hours from now, but tomorrow is a new day.

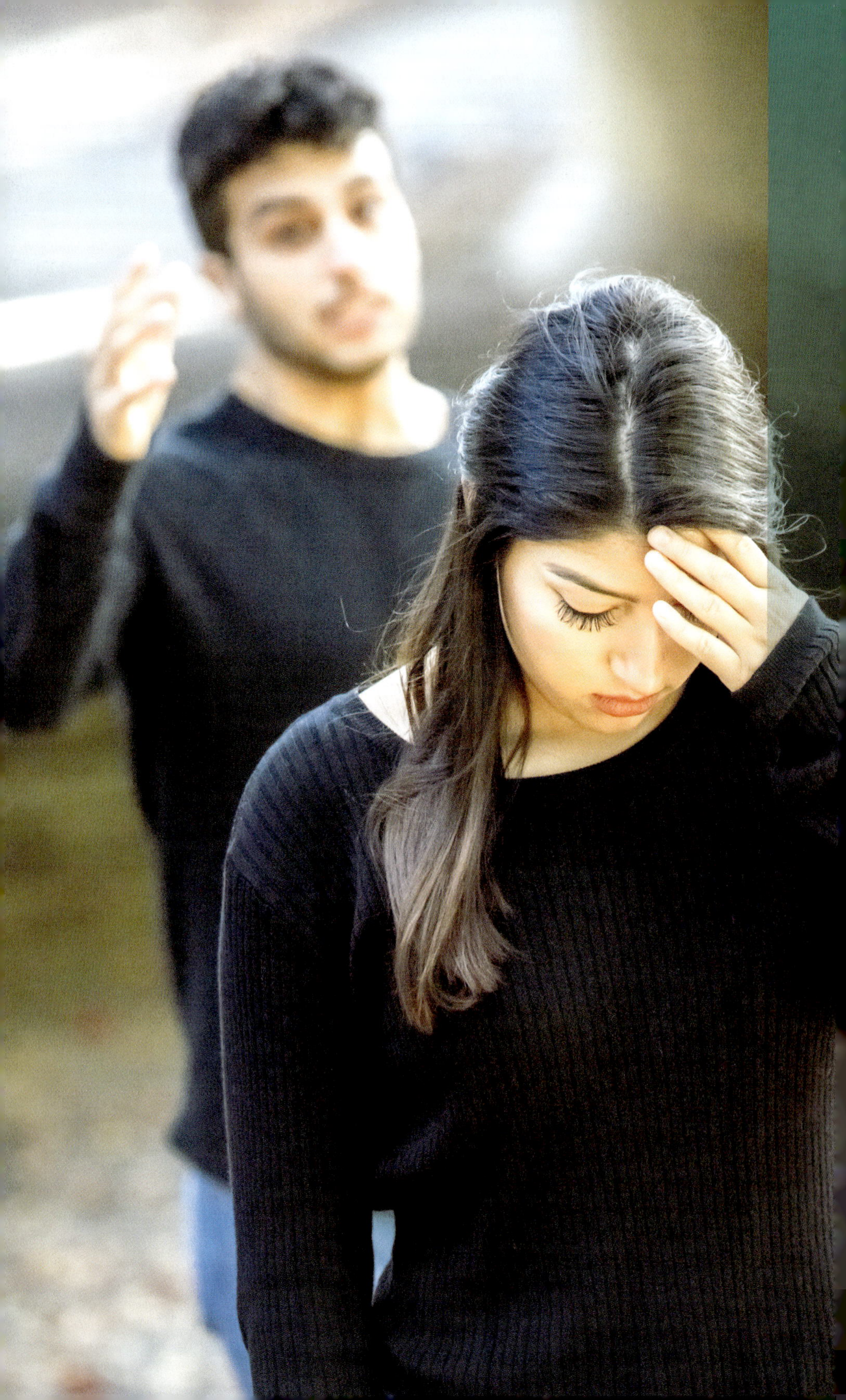

CHAPTER SIX

ABUSIVE RELATIONSHIPS

Having an argument is normal. But there's a huge distinction between a disagreement every now and then—or even a serious fight—and something much more menacing and problematic. Though it sounds like a no-brainer, it bears repeating: abuse is not healthy and should be avoided no matter what the circumstances are. But how do you tell the difference between behavior that's abusive and a fight that's just a little louder than usual?

Most people equate abuse with physical violence. While that's often the case, not all abuse is physical. According to the National Domestic Violence Hotline, domestic abuse is defined as behaviors used by one person to exert power and control over another person in a close relationship. That includes more obvious actions such as threats, intimidation, and repeated belligerent behavior. It can also be something more subtle, such as monitoring emails and text messages or controlling the clothes one's partner wears and the friends he or she chooses. If your partner is making you feel afraid for any reason or is preventing you from doing something you want to do in a hurtful or physically aggressive way, you might be in an abusive relationship.

> If your partner is making you feel afraid for any reason or is preventing you from doing something you want to do... you might be in an abusive relationship.

So, what do you do if you suspect your partner is being abusive? Are there signs to look out for? And most importantly, how do you get out of an abusive relationship? Unfortunately, Mandy found herself in the beginnings of an abusive relationship.

MANDY'S STORY

Ever since the beginning of her freshman year in high school, Mandy had her eye on Isaac. Tall and totally handsome, he was considered the catch of his junior class. So, when he smiled at Mandy at a basketball game, she actually turned around to find out which girl he was looking at behind her. And when he stopped by her locker the next day to introduce himself, she almost fainted. How could *he* like *her*? He was definitely out of her league.

Over the next couple weeks, they got past "hello" and actually started talking. Eventually, Isaac asked Mandy out, and the two started dating. For those first few months, Mandy thought things were great. She loved how he always commented on her looks, telling her she should wear skirts more often to show off her legs. When he suggested that she dye her hair a lighter color, she felt slightly uncomfortable—after all, she loved her dark brown curls. Still, their relationship was new, so she decided to run with it. In the end, they had a fun afternoon in her bathroom trying to dye her hair from one of those boxes you buy at the drugstore. Isaac must have really cared about her if he was showing so much interest in the way she presented herself, right?

***

After about four months, Mandy and Isaac settled into a routine. He would walk her to the subway, and she would text him when she got home. Sometimes they'd message each other first thing in the morning when they woke up. On the weekends, she started spending less time with her friends so she could hang out and snuggle with Isaac or watch when he played hoops in the park with his boys.

But one weekend, Mandy woke up thinking it had been way too long since she'd had any girl time. Serendipitously, she checked her phone and saw a message from her best friend, Kat. "I miss you!" it read. "Let's get together. Dahlia and I are headed out to grab a bite. Take a break from your man and come with!"

> **TALK ABOUT IT**
>
> ▪ Have you ever dated someone you thought was "out of your league"? How did that feel?
>
> ▪ If you were Mandy, would you have dyed your hair after Isaac suggested doing so? Why or why not?
>
> ▪ Do you think Isaac's interest in Mandy's appearance is flattering? How would you feel if your partner made suggestions about the way you looked or dressed?

It sounded like exactly what Mandy was in the mood for. She texted Isaac to tell him her plans and that she would see him the next day for their usual Sunday run. Then she went to get ready. About a half hour later, she heard the buzzer ring. Her mother yelled back to her, "Mandy, Isaac's here to see you."

Mandy ran down the hall and saw Isaac at the door. He had a basketball under his arm. "I know you said you were going out with your friends. But I thought it'd be more fun for us to settle our one-on-one tournament to see who's the ultimate hoops champion," he said.

Mandy felt her lungs deflate. More than anything, she wanted to hang out with her friends. But she also didn't want to disappoint Isaac. She hesitated for a second, then smiled and grabbed the ball out of his hand.

"Sure. Let me go put on my sneakers. I can see the girls at school on Monday," she said.

***

Isaac creamed Mandy on the court, but she put up a good hustle. The next day, they ran together in the park, and Mandy beat his mile by two minutes. She got a bunch of texts from Kat and her other friends but didn't respond. The more her phone chimed with incoming messages, the more irritated Isaac got.

Finally, he grabbed the phone, entered in her unlock code, and typed in "Leave me alone. I'm hanging out with Isaac."

TALK ABOUT IT

- Why do you think Mandy chose to play hoops with Isaac instead of hanging out with her friends?
- If you were Mandy, would you have gone to hang out with your friends instead? Why or why not?
- Do you think it was fair of Isaac to make Mandy choose between him and her friends? Why or why not?

Then he slipped the phone into his bag and wouldn't give it back to Mandy for the rest of the day.

"It's pretty lame that they're making you feel guilty about hanging out with your boyfriend," he said. "I bet they're just jealous. I'm not cool with you hanging out with them anymore. They're just dragging you down."

Suddenly, something clicked in Mandy's head. She was fine

Then he slipped the phone into his bag and wouldn't give it back to Mandy for the rest of the day.

with taking fashion advice from Isaac and even changing her appearance—slightly—as a fun experiment. But giving up her friends? For him? That was too much. Mandy tried to calmly explain to Isaac how his behavior made her feel, but he would hear none of it. Instead, he spent the rest of the afternoon berating her, telling her that she was lucky to be dating him and that she would be nothing without him.

***

The next day at lunchtime, Mandy sat with Kat and the rest of her friend group in the cafeteria like she usually did. But the mood was tense. "So, I don't think we need to have a ginormous conversation about this, but this thing with Isaac is getting a little out of hand," Kat said. "We get that he loves you and all, but we do too."

"I love you guys too! But I don't think Isaac loves me," Mandy said. "You're right. Isaac has been really controlling. He even wanted me to stop being friends with you. After our run yesterday, we ended up spending the whole walk home arguing, and he got really mean. It kind of freaked me out. I was so exhausted from all the fighting that I told him I needed some space and time to think."

"What did he say?" Kat asked, taken aback.

"Let's just say he wasn't happy at all," Mandy said. "But I was at my front door when I said it and just went inside. Thankfully my mom was right there, so he didn't press it." Mandy looked shaken from the experience. When the girls saw how upset she was, they leaned in and gave her a giant, collective hug.

TALK ABOUT IT

- Do you think it's healthy for a romantic partner to monitor your texts or respond on your behalf? Why or why not?
- Do you think Kat was right to speak out about Mandy's behavior?
- Do you think it's best to share your opinion with your friends even if it might hurt them, or is it better to keep quiet?
- What do you think of Mandy's response to Isaac's behavior in the last scene? What would you have done?

ASK THE EXPERT

Interpreting signs of abuse in a relationship can sometimes be tricky, especially when it involves someone you care about. But there is a big difference between making helpful suggestions and being way too demanding. If your partner is monitoring your texts or emails; preventing you from making your own decisions; or telling you what to wear, when to wear it, and who you can hang out with, that is abusive and unhealthy. Your partner should be your equal, not your controller.

Abuse can happen to anyone regardless of gender, class, race, age, or background. It's important to learn how to spot and address abusive behavior when it starts. Though it's not always the case, abuse often starts out as emotional manipulation and becomes physical later. Going too long without addressing the abuse can lead to worse emotional or physical effects. According to Break the Cycle, an organization geared toward preventing domestic and dating violence, some abuse victims become so accustomed to hearing personal attacks that they become depressed, anxious, or doubt their own ability to take care of themselves. When those types of feelings take hold, it can become more difficult to seek help.

For these reasons, it's crucial that you deal with abuse immediately. Set boundaries with your partner. Define what kind of behavior and language is acceptable and what isn't. If your partner can't hear your concerns or meet your expectations, it's time to either seek help for your relationship or move on.

GET **HEALTHY**

- If your partner seems controlling, have a talk explaining what you will and will not put up with. Be firm but not confrontational.
- Develop a safety plan for leaving an abusive relationship. Enlist the help of someone you trust.
- Call the National Domestic Violence Hotline (1-800-799-7233 [SAFE]) if the matter is serious or you just want advice. It's free 24 hours a day, seven days a week.
- Remember that if you are being abused, it is never your fault. You never deserve to be treated that way.

THE LAST WORD FROM **ALEXIS**

It's easy to get swept up in a romantic relationship. But dealing with an abusive partner doesn't just make you feel totally worthless; it can also be dangerous. Protect yourself by balancing your beau time with friend time. Your pals are usually looking out for your best interests and know what's up. If your best friend says something seems off, she's probably right. If you think you're in an unhealthy or abusive relationship, talk to an adult who might be able to help. And most importantly, remember that you're beautiful just the way you are. If your partner comes to you with a list of things you need to change about yourself, maybe it's time to kick him or her to the curb. If it's more serious than that, do your best to get out of that relationship as soon as possible.

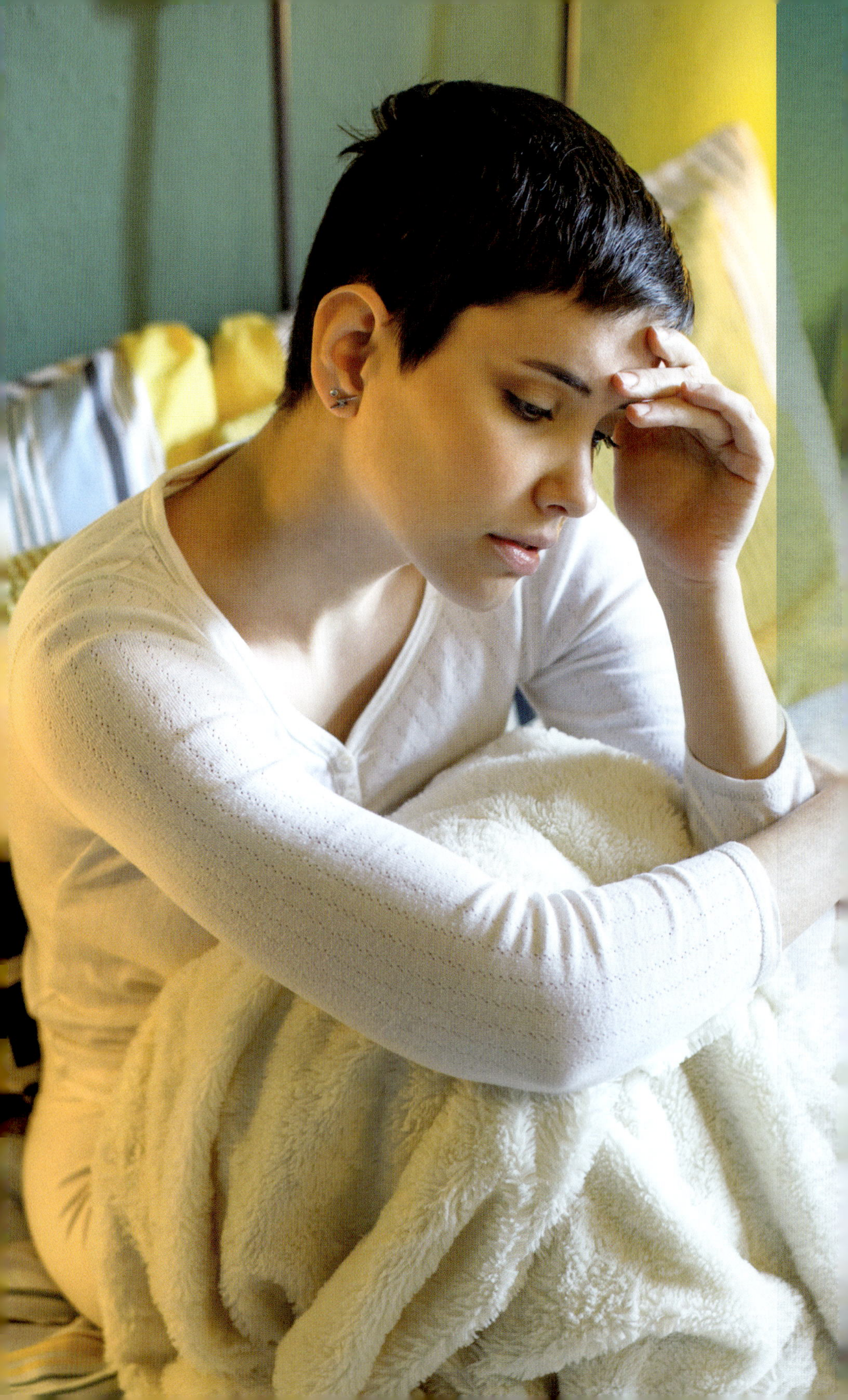

CHAPTER SEVEN

IS IT TIME TO BREAK UP?

Giving up is hard, especially when it has to do with something so potentially joyous and life affirming as being in love. Believe me, I hear you. All those fun dates together, that giddy time after you realized you liked each other and wanted to be a team, all the hugging and kissing and mushy romantic moments. No matter how you feel now, those things were real. They happened. You felt blissful and on top of the world—until you didn't.

Sometimes staying in a relationship after it has started to sour is the worst choice you can make. Working through problems day after day without any relief or improvement can be a real soul-sucker. The hard truth is that prolonging an inevitable split prevents you from being happy, productive, strong individuals who are probably better off apart than together.

So how do you know when it's time to move on? What are some telltale signs that you should probably call it quits? And perhaps more importantly, how do you break up with someone and not have him or her hate you, or how do you not fall apart when your partner dumps you? Serena found herself in this situation when her relationship with her girlfriend, Eliza, started going downhill.

SERENA'S STORY

Serena was what her friends liked to call extra-extroverted. She didn't just like going out—she liked going above and beyond.

When she went out dancing with her friends, she wasn't afraid to go up to complete strangers and strike up conversations while doing some smooth dance moves—she'd even go up to girls she had crushes on. Basically, her idea of a nightmare was staying home on a Friday night and watching a movie. That is, until she met Eliza.

Eliza was your classic bookish introvert. She loved doing yoga or spending time in the old county library by her house. In fact, that's where she and Serena met, when Serena was looking for a public bathroom while out on a run. Serena thought Eliza was cute and immediately asked her out on a date. They had been dating ever since.

The first three months of their relationship were a total whirlwind. Serena tried to introduce Eliza to all sorts of things she never would've dreamed of doing, such as

TALK ABOUT IT

- **Serena gets Eliza to do things that are outside her comfort zone. Do you think this is a good thing? Why or why not?**
- **Have you ever dated or been interested in someone who is totally different from you? Do you think it's true that opposites attract?**

> The first three months of their relationship were a total whirlwind.

taking a trapeze class together. Serena loved it, but it made Eliza feel totally nauseated.

"You're a natural!" Serena yelled back, watching her girlfriend from the ground. "Next week, I'm forcing you to go snowboarding. No excuses!"

Eliza inwardly groaned. She hated anything having to do with speed and sports, but she wasn't going to tell Serena that. Serena didn't like taking no for an answer.

> Serena didn't like taking no for an answer.

***

Eight months later, Eliza still hadn't gone snowboarding with Serena, but that hadn't stopped Serena from asking her to go every weekend during the season. In fact, more often than not, Serena felt like she had to beg or drag Eliza along to do anything remotely interesting. All Eliza wanted to do was play board games on Saturday night. Serena was starting to feel like she was dating her grandmother.

One day after school, Serena was sitting on the hood of her car in the school parking lot. She was talking to Monisha, a friend from her class she had started spending more time with. In the past few months, when Eliza had bailed on date night after date night to stay home and read, Serena had called Monisha, who jumped at the chance to fill in. Monisha had also become a shoulder to cry on when Serena had problems in her love life.

"I don't know what's wrong with us. She used to be at least willing to take chances. Now she's just kind of a bore," Serena complained. "I've asked her what she wants to do instead, but she always has weird suggestions, like knitting. I mean, knitting? Then she just says she'll do whatever I want next time, but she never does."

"Yeah, I've noticed that you two don't seem to be as close as you used to. How long has this been going on?" Monisha asked.

"For more than eight months," Serena responded. "And anytime I go near her, she goes stiff or pulls away. I feel like I've done something wrong, but I have no idea what it is. I've spent more time with you this week than I have with her in the past five months! It's crazy."

"Hmm. Maybe you should talk to her about it," Monisha suggested. "Or maybe you two need some time apart?"

"I have tried talking over and over, but it's like she just won't talk about her feelings," Serena said, sadly. "And yeah, I honestly think it might be time for us to go our separate ways."

TALK ABOUT IT

- **What are some healthy things you noticed about Serena and Eliza's relationship? What are some potential red flags?**
- **Do you tell your friends about things that are going wrong in your relationship, or do you share just the good stuff? Why?**

***

That night, Serena thought a lot about what Monisha had said. Serena had given her relationship ample time to improve, but Eliza didn't seem to want to compromise or change. The next morning, she texted Eliza to see whether she had any time to talk.

They grabbed some coffee and a few bagels and went to their favorite park. The conversation started out awkwardly.

Eventually, Eliza interrupted Serena's babbling. "Uh, Serena. Did you bring me here to talk about something? It's kind of cold," she said.

"Oh, right. So, I guess I don't really know what is going on, but I don't think our relationship is working," Serena said. "I've tried to talk to you about it for a long time, but every time I try, you shut me down or change the subject. I don't know what else to do, and I don't think I want to be in this relationship anymore."

Eliza was quiet for a long time. Serena could tell she was holding back tears. "Are you breaking up with me?" Eliza asked.

"Eliza, I love you, but I don't think we're really right for each other. I mean, I love to go 24-7, and you're just content to read or meditate. Maybe it worked in the beginning because everything was new and exciting, but now I feel like you just resent me for wanting to spend time with you," Serena said.

> Eliza was quiet for a long time. Serena could tell she was holding back tears.

"Well, I guess I haven't loved that every time I've suggested something, you've just seemed bored or have spent the whole

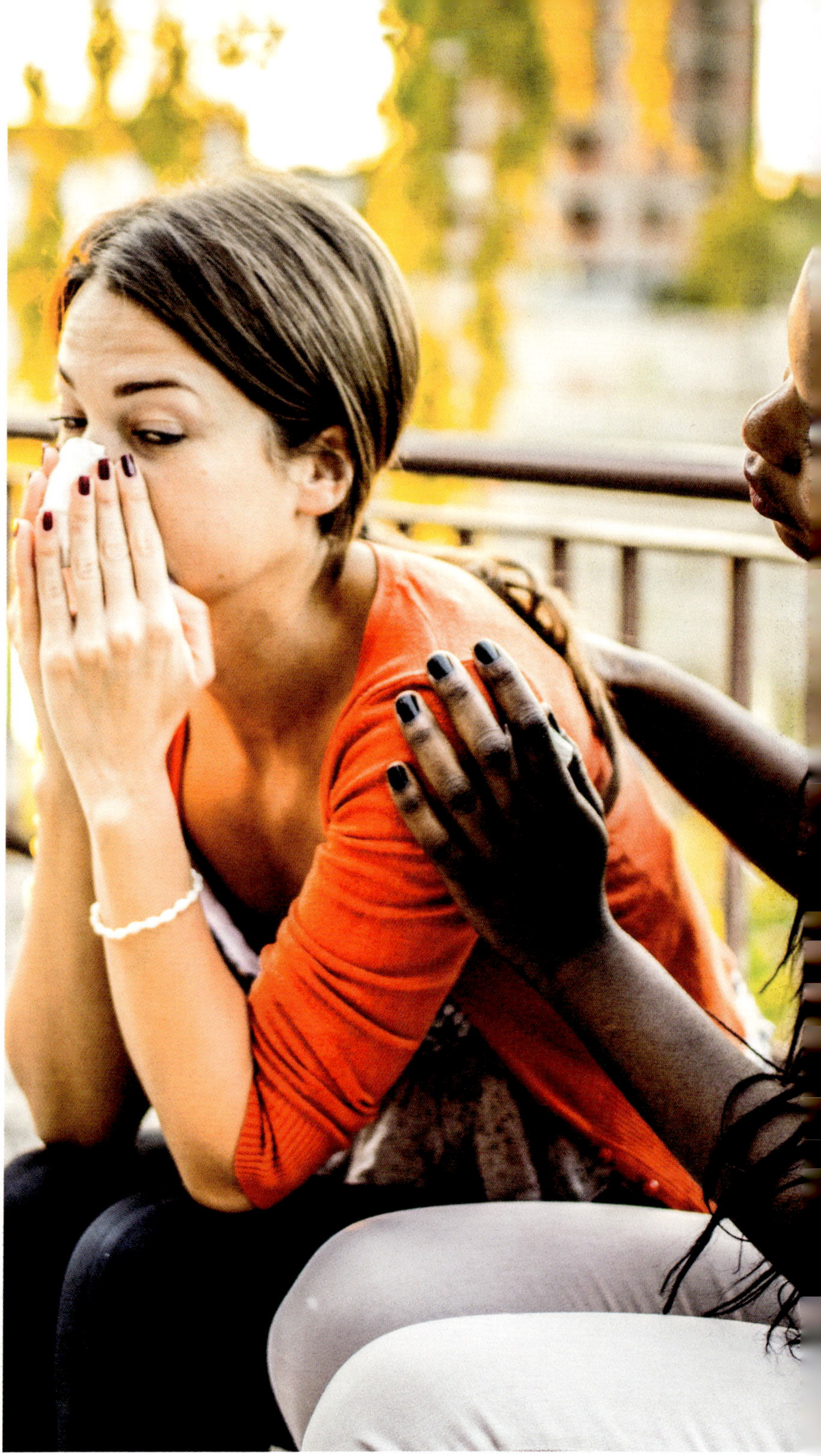

time looking at the clock until it's over. That doesn't feel great," Eliza responded.

"Yeah, I guess you're right about that. I do kind of hate knitting," Serena said with a sad smile. "It's awful, but we shouldn't have to become different people in order for this to work, right? I think we just need some time apart for now. If you want, we can take a break and talk again in a month to see where we're at."

Eliza sniffed, blew her nose, and nodded her head. "OK. Let's see where we are after a month," she said.

TALK ABOUT IT

- Have you ever broken up with someone or been dumped? If so, how did it feel? Was it the right decision in the end?
- If you've been through a breakup before, are there things you wish you had done differently?
- Do you think it's easier to be dumped or to be the person who initiates the breakup? Why?
- How do you think Serena and Eliza handled the breakup conversation?

ASK THE EXPERT

Love and romance are delicate things. They need to be nurtured and given time and attention every day. If you're feeling like you're not quite getting along with your partner or that your relationship might be on the rocks, you're probably not imagining it. In most situations, there are surefire signs that a couple isn't as healthy as it ought to be.

For example, if you're feeling disengaged, uninterested, or stuck, that's not ideal. Knowing that your needs aren't being met and yet feeling obligated to stay with your partner anyway is like a disaster waiting to happen. But if both members of the couple are willing to put in the work to try to save the relationship—by talking through what needs to change, making healthy compromises in order to grow together, or possibly going to couples counseling if necessary—then it's possible things can improve with time.

In other situations, it might be best to acknowledge your differences and move on. If your physical routine has changed as a couple, that's something to examine. Lack of intimacy with and attraction to your partner is problematic. If either you or your partner is seeking emotional or physical fulfillment from people outside your monogamous relationship, it's an indication that it's probably time to break up or at least take time apart. Whatever you do, don't ignore the situation. Stay strong and talk to each other. Address the problem head-on. If you can't work through it, then end your relationship with grace and dignity. Don't forget to get support from your friends and family if you need it. You'd do the same for them.

GET HEALTHY

- Pay attention to your relationship. If you sense there are issues, honestly work through them and stay watchful of signs it might be time to split.
- If you've both tried to fix the relationship and it still isn't working, don't wait to end the relationship.
- Do the breakup in person and in private. Breaking up in a public place doesn't allow either of you to express emotion comfortably, and splitting over text is inconsiderate.
- Take some time apart from your ex-girlfriend or boyfriend. Moving immediately into friendship causes uncertainty and prevents relearning independence.

THE LAST WORD FROM ALEXIS

Slogging through a faltering relationship stinks. Breaking up can feel even worse. If you're the one who gets dumped, it's like every day is the saddest day on the planet and you've got "your song" on repeat. If you're the one who breaks up with someone, it's nearly impossible not to feel guilty about hurting another person. But try not to be too hard on yourself. Tell yourself you tried your best and move forward. And if I may, one last tip from yours truly: after breaking up, don't start dating again right away. Untangle your emotions. Take some time to get to know yourself again as a single person. Try to learn from what didn't work in your previous relationship so as not to repeat the pattern.

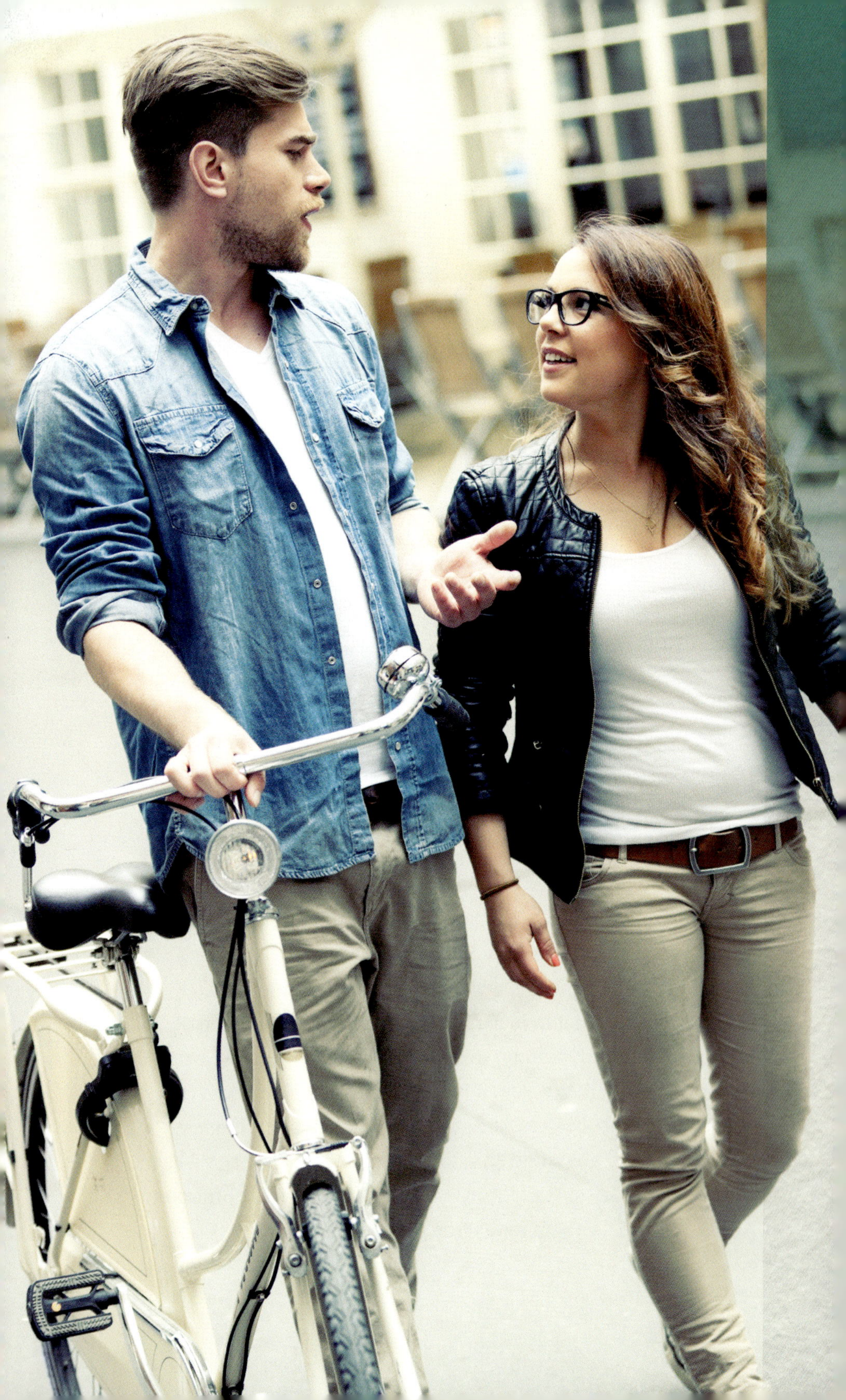

CHAPTER EIGHT

COMMITMENT 101

You and your partner have been going strong for three years now. You're old pros at communicating openly. You've mastered the art of compromise. You've had the occasional spat (and sometimes a full-on fight) and come through it to the other side. In short, you're the real deal.

So, why do you feel so . . . stuck? Bored? So terribly humdrum and blah? It's not that you've stopped loving your partner. After all, you couldn't imagine life without him or her. Instead, it's more like all the pizzazz, excitement, and surprise has slowly but steadily leaked out of your relationship. Is there any hope of getting it back?

Let me fill you in on an often-misunderstood truth about romance. The reality is that long-term relationships don't usually play out on cloud nine. They might start there, but that amped-up energy usually dissipates as you get to know each other and become more comfortable being yourselves. With that said, there are ways to spice up your relationship to prevent it from devolving into a giant snooze fest. Sonia and Carter acknowledged the monotony in being a long-term couple and set out to beat it.

SONIA'S STORY

Sonia and a bunch of her friends were hanging out in her backyard, drinking slushies and gossiping, when one of her closest friends looked at her buzzing phone and let out a cheer.

"Yes! He asked me!" Christina screamed. "I have a date with Sudeesh. It's on. It's on. It's ON!"

Everyone let out a collective whoop. It had been a full year since Christina had started nursing her crush on Sudeesh. During that time, he'd never asked her out officially—until now.

"He is already being so romantic!" Christina squealed. "Just now, he texted me saying he wanted to take me out for 'an enchanted evening full of surprises.' He won't even tell me what we're doing so I can figure out what to wear!"

Just then, Sonia's phone buzzed. It was Carter, her boyfriend of three years.

"Speaking of surprises, what are you and Carter up to this weekend, Sonia? Laundry?" Christina asked. Everyone laughed.

Sonia threw a potato chip at Christina. "Very funny," she said. "But, yeah, actually. Probably more of the same. We haven't had a super romantic date in over a year. In fact, the closest we got is watching the Super Bowl together in our sweatpants."

The girls burst out laughing once more. But even though Sonia was smiling too, she secretly wasn't amused. The truth was that she and Carter had been coasting for over a year without anything new

> **TALK ABOUT IT**
>
> - Have you ever been in a long-term relationship? If so, how did it change over time?
> - Do you ever get envious when friends ramble on about romantic dates or how well their relationships are going? Why or why not?

Even though Sonia was smiling too, she secretly wasn't amused.

on the horizon. How come he wasn't being super romantic like Sudeesh was with Christina?

***

On Monday morning at school, all everyone talked about was Christina's romantic date. Sudeesh had taken her to a small amusement park a few towns over. It turned out he was a pro at playing the ring toss and won her a huge stuffed teddy bear. Then he took her to a fancy seafood restaurant for dinner and picked up the bill. He didn't even try to kiss her until he dropped her off at home just in time for curfew—the perfect gentleman.

Sonia had to admit the date was a slam dunk. But she couldn't shake the feeling that her relationship was boring in comparison. Was Carter even capable of doing something like that for her? For the next week, she barely responded to his texts and phone calls. She even tried flirting with other guys to see how it felt.

On Friday, Carter cornered Sonia as she was heading toward chemistry class. "Babe, can I talk to you?" he said to her. They leaned against some lockers. "Did I do something wrong? I feel like you've been ignoring me all week. Maybe we can talk at our usual spot tonight?"

"Ugh, our *usual* spot. Can't we ever do anything interesting?" Sonia said to Carter, clearly disgusted. "Fine. Whatever. See you at the diner at our *usual* time."

***

> **TALK ABOUT IT**
>
> ▪ Do you ever compare your relationship with those of your friends? If so, is it helpful?
>
> ▪ Sonia tried flirting with other guys when she was in a rut with Carter. Why do you think she did that? Do you think that behavior is acceptable?

Later, at the diner, Carter waited for Sonia in their usual booth. He had already ordered her favorite: a banana split with extra peanuts and hot fudge, no whipped cream. He had also placed a tiny daffodil by her plate. When Sonia arrived, she was in a grumpy mood. But the flower made her smile. A little.

Carter started right in before she could take off her coat. "Babe, I'm not sure what I did, but I'm sorry for whatever it is. Do you want to tell me what's wrong?"

Sonia frowned and tried to stand firm in her grumpy ground. But when she looked at Carter's face, all she could see was his affection for her. She took a deep breath and sighed. "No, I should be the one who's apologizing. I've been a jerk to you all week," she said. "It's just that Christina was going on and on about her date with Sudeesh, and I kept thinking about how we hadn't done anything like that for a long time. Like, when did our relationship get so boring?"

> "When did our relationship get so boring?"

"Boring?" Carter asked. "I didn't realize you thought our relationship was boring. How long have you been unhappy?"

"I'm not unhappy, Carter. You know I love you. I just think we need some excitement in our relationship. I mean, look at us now. We're sitting in the same booth at the same diner eating the same food," Sonia said.

"I thought you liked this diner," Carter replied.

"I do!" Sonia responded. "Just maybe not *every* time. I mean, the flower was a nice touch. What if we both tried to do

TALK ABOUT IT

- **What do you like better: the thrill and crazy energy at the beginning of a relationship or later on in the relationship when you know what to expect?**
- **Do you think it's possible to have a relationship that will last for a long time? Why or why not?**
- **What are some ways to spice up a relationship?**
- **In the end, Sonia and Carter talked through their problem. How do you think that conversation went?**

something like the flower, but on a larger scale?"

"You mean, plan little surprises for each other every once in a while?" Carter asked, a smile creeping onto his face.

"Exactly. Like when we each least expect it. It might be fun," Sonia said.

"Well, you know I *do* enjoy a challenge," Carter said.

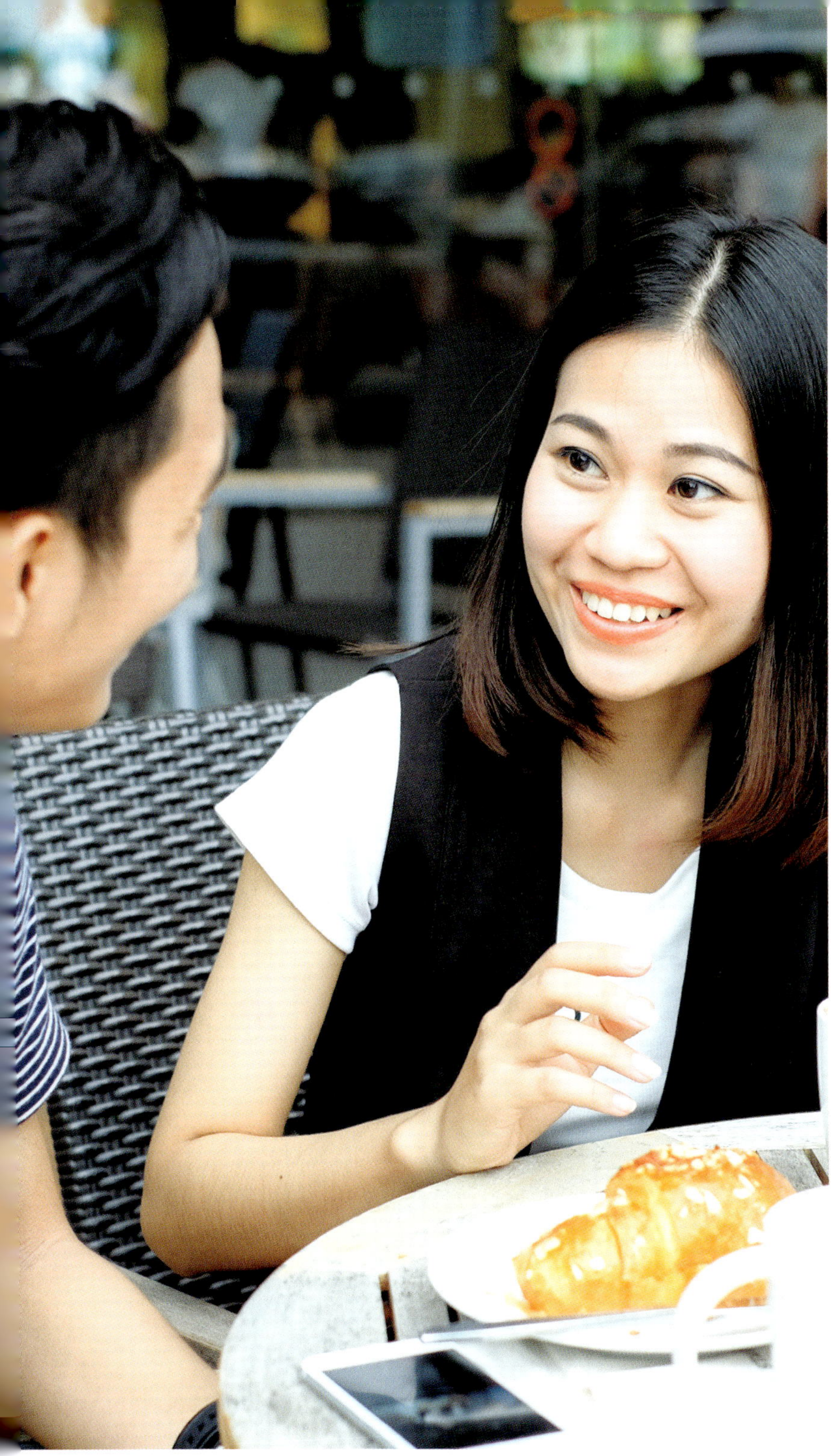

ASK THE EXPERT

Falling in love is so magical. It's like no other emotion in the world. Because the object of your affection also appreciates everything about you and adores spending time with you, it's easy to feel confident, beautiful, smart, and like the person you've always wanted to be. But after the initial elation fades, the newness wears off, and the honeymoon phase ends, most long-term relationships settle into a routine, as Sonia and Carter's did. Things like work, school, and day-to-day responsibilities take precedence again. Romance gets relegated to the back burner. Sometimes what was once so electrifying becomes monotonous and stale.

But just because you've been with your partner for a long time doesn't mean your romance is doomed to dullness. There are plenty of ways to keep the spark alive while you grow and explore your lives together. Why not do something out of your mutual comfort zone? New activities not only keep things exciting but also provide opportunities to explore and grow within a relationship. Who knows? Keeping each other on your collective toes might be just the thing that keeps you going for the long haul. Experiment a bit and see what happens. And most importantly, don't forget to express your gratitude and love for each other. It might sound corny or seem like it would lose its meaning over time, but expressing love for your partner (and hearing it in return) should never get old, no matter how many times it happens.

GET **HEALTHY**

- If things have started to fizzle in your relationship, spice up your routine. Do something new.
- Try switching roles within the relationship. If one person is always the planner, give the other person a shot at taking the reins.
- Express your feelings for each other. If you love your partner, then say, "I love you." Find other ways to show you care.
- Cheating or flirting with other people is off-limits unless you have an open relationship. It's disrespectful, makes your partner feel bad, and may permanently damage your relationship.

THE LAST WORD FROM **ALEXIS**

Are you in a long-term relationship and thinking to yourself, "Is this it?" Believe me, I've been there. It's depressing. But this kind of self-analysis should also tell you something very important: you're missing something in your connection, and it's time to do something about it. Don't be like Sonia and ignore the problem until there's a fight. Be the strong, insightful girl you are and take on the challenge. Get creative. Plan a surprise weekend jaunt! Write your partner sweet notes. The sky's the limit. Most importantly, remember to have fun while you're spicing up your love life. Maybe a little whimsy is all you need!

A SECOND LOOK

Now that you've had a chance to go through some of the stories in this book, I hope reading about other teens' relationships has been invigorating and thought-provoking. I also hope some of their successes and missteps inspire you to get out there and try some moves of your own. You are strong, smart, beautiful, and totally unique. Any guy or gal would be lucky to fall in love with you.

As you move through the world of crushes, dating, true romance, and sex, keep an open mind. When it comes to finding a partner, look for someone with whom you feel comfortable. Being comfortable with a romantic partner means you can be your truest self, whether that's cracking your corniest jokes, sharing your deepest thoughts, or exploring your sexuality. It also means you two can have different friend groups, different opinions, and even different backgrounds and know that it's all right. After all, in my book, the best couples are not two halves of one whole but two complete individuals who are joining together to create an even bigger, more awesome union.

If you're coming out of a relationship and didn't handle the breakup in the best way, try not to give yourself too hard a time. The truth is we all make mistakes, and it's never too late to do better. If you've had someone break up with you and you can't seem to get over it, don't beat yourself up either! Girls the world over have gone through the process and come out on the other side. Maybe it's time to grab some of your best friends and hang out with them for a while until you've healed and are ready to get back in the saddle.

Most importantly, whether you're a high schooler or grown adult, healthy romantic relationships are possible for *all* types of people, regardless of their sexuality or gender. Love is made for you. Don't let anyone tell you differently. Yes, the journey to Super Couple might feel hard at times. Yes, it might even feel too good to be true at others. But every bit of it is worth it. I promise.

XOXO,
ALEXIS

PAY IT FORWARD

A healthy romantic relationship is all about compassion, compromise, and confidence. Discovering what makes you feel your best is a journey that changes throughout your life. Now that you know what to focus on, you can pay it forward to a friend too. Remember the Get Healthy tips throughout this book, and then take these steps to get healthy and get going.

1. **Start every relationship by loving yourself. Being comfortable with who you are, what you need, and what you desire is essential. Doing so brings the best you to the relationship.**

2. **If you're having sex, make sure it's always protected. Use a condom to protect against sexually transmitted diseases. Use your preferred method of birth control to protect against unwanted pregnancy. Talk to a parent, guardian, or health-care provider about which birth control option is right for you.**

3. **Know the signs of unhealthy fighting. Unhealthy fighting involves name-calling, poor listening, and blaming.**

4. **Look out for signs of abusive behavior. It can be physical, emotional, or mental. If your partner is trying to control you**

or force you to change or is hurting you in any way, this is considered abuse. Get out of the relationship immediately and report it to an authority figure if you need help.

5. If you're overwhelmed by emotions, why not write it all down? Keeping a journal can give you much-needed perspective.

6. Express your feelings for your partner in any way you know how. A little affection goes a long way.

7. If you and your partner seem to want different things, examine your relationship to see whether it's salvageable. If you both agree it is, try to work through your problems honestly, respectfully, and without blame so that each person feels heard.

8. If it's time to break up, do so decisively and right away. Waiting too long or offering false hope just complicates matters in the long run and makes it more difficult to separate.

9. Remember that you hold the key to your own castle. Being in love is wonderful. But if you haven't found your partner yet or the one you're with isn't the right one for you, don't worry. From my experience, love comes around when you least expect it.

GLOSSARY

belligerent
Hostile, aggressive, or combative.

consent
The process of obtaining explicit and clear permission to cross someone's physical boundaries. Consent must be given without pressure, guilt, or manipulation; refers only to the specific activity for which it's obtained; and can be taken back at any time.

contraception
Methods used to prevent pregnancy.

extroverted
Outgoing and socially confident.

introvert
Someone who prefers spending time alone or in low-stimulation environments.

monogamous
Having a romantic relationship with only one person at one time.

monotony
The same thing over and over; a lack of variety that often leads to boredom.

morning-after pill
A pill that can be taken after sex to interfere with pregnancy.

mortifying
Very embarrassing or humiliating.

puberty
The beginning of physical maturity when a person becomes capable of reproducing sexually.

reciprocated
Returned in the same way.

stag
With a group of friends instead of with a date, especially when going to a dance.

tumultuous
Confused or disorderly; filled with upheaval.

visceral
Relating to deep emotions and gut feelings rather than intellect.

ADDITIONAL RESOURCES

SELECTED BIBLIOGRAPHY

Breit, Carly. "This Is the Best Way to Fight with Your Partner, According to Psychologists." *TIME*, 24 Sept. 2018, time.com.

"Teens and Sex: Protecting Your Teen's Sexual Health." *Mayo Clinic*, 3 Aug. 2017, mayoclinic.org.

"What Is Domestic Violence?" *National Domestic Violence Hotline*, n.d., thehotline.org.

FURTHER READINGS

Ford, Jeanne Marie. *Understanding Reproductive Health*. Abdo, 2021.

Planned Parenthood. *In Case You're Curious*. Viva Editions, 2019.

Rayne, Karen. *Girl: Love, Sex, Romance, and Being You*. Magination Press, 2017.

ONLINE RESOURCES

Booklinks NONFICTION NETWORK
FREE! ONLINE NONFICTION RESOURCES

To learn more about healthy romantic relationships, please visit **abdobooklinks.com** or scan this QR code. These links are routinely monitored and updated to provide the most current information available.

MORE INFORMATION

For more information on this subject, contact or visit the following organizations:

Advocates for Youth

1325 G St. NW, Suite 980
Washington, DC 20005
advocatesforyouth.org
202-419-3420

Advocates for Youth delivers sexual health information and services to adolescents in need, regardless of gender, race, or class.

Break the Cycle

P.O. Box 811334
Los Angeles, CA 90081
breakthecycle.org
424-265-7346

Break the Cycle is a nonprofit organization that aims to end dating violence and helps victims of domestic abuse by connecting them with valuable resources.

Girls Inc.

120 Wall St., Eighteenth Floor
New York, NY 10005
girlsinc.org
212-509-2000

This national organization focuses on long-term mentoring relationships and research-based programming to help girls grow up healthy, independent, and educated.

INDEX

abuse, 7, 67–77
advice, 18, 36, 53, 74, 77
anger, 57–58, 65
appearance, 70, 74
attraction, 9, 18, 81, 88

behavior, 9, 19, 26, 58, 62, 64–65, 67, 74–77, 95
birth control, 49, 51, 54–55
boundaries, 55, 76
Break the Cycle, 76
breakups, 7, 33, 79–89

changes, 9, 33, 36, 64, 74, 77, 84, 88, 93
cheating, 101
comfort zone, 81, 100
commitment, 21, 29, 31, 33, 42–43, 46, 91–101
communication, 22, 30, 42, 55, 91
compassion, 9, 34
compromise, 7, 64–65, 84, 88, 91
condoms, 52, 54–55
confidence, 24, 42–43, 46, 100
conflict, 6, 57, 64
confusion, 13, 26, 42
control, 7, 54, 67, 75–77
conversation, 38, 41–42, 57, 75, 81, 85, 87, 98
couples, 16, 33, 43, 57, 64, 88, 92
crushes, 6, 9–11, 12, 14, 17, 18–19, 21–22, 28, 81, 92

dating, 12–14, 21–22, 24, 30–31, 33–34, 46–47, 62, 69, 70, 74, 79, 81–82, 89, 92–96
decisions, 6–7, 14–16, 19, 21–22, 25, 30–31, 33–34, 48, 52, 54, 69, 76, 87
defensiveness, 64–65
defining the relationship, 33–43
disagreement, 57, 64, 67

embarrassment, 6, 9, 43, 47, 49–50
emotions, 18, 45, 64, 76, 88–89, 100
energy, 14, 91, 98
exclusivity, 21, 42–43
excuses, 27, 82
expression, 42–43, 54, 57, 89, 100–101

fears, 38, 42, 68, 81
fighting, 57–58, 63–65, 67, 75, 91, 101
first time, 6, 24, 36, 46–47, 54
flirting, 33, 60, 95, 101
friendship, 6, 10–12, 14, 17–19, 23–24, 26, 30–31, 34, 46–47, 51–52, 54, 59, 61, 63, 67, 70, 72, 74–75, 77, 80–82, 84, 89, 92, 93, 95

hanging out, 21, 26, 29, 31, 33–38, 41, 63, 70, 72–73, 76, 92
health, 6–7, 21, 45, 49, 54, 57–58, 63–64, 67, 75–77, 84, 88
heartache, 30, 40
hobbies, 30
homecoming dance, 12–14
honeymoon phase, 100
human immunodeficiency virus (HIV), 45

110

human papillomavirus (HPV), 45
hurt feelings, 31, 63, 68, 75, 89

infatuation, 18
interests, 6, 12, 31, 41, 70, 77, 81–82, 88, 95
intimacy, 45–46, 54–55, 88
intimidation, 67
irritation, 72

jealousy, 62–64, 73

kissing, 24, 63, 79, 95

love, 6–7, 11, 14, 18–19, 30, 34, 41, 43, 46, 65, 69, 75, 79, 81–83, 85, 88, 91, 96, 100–101

mistakes, 7, 65
mixed messages, 29
monitoring, 67, 75–76

National Domestic Violence Hotline, 67, 77
nervousness, 14, 16, 19, 21, 41, 47, 48, 51
nurse, 52–53

obsessing, 12, 21
options, 22, 31, 55
overthinking, 15, 22

parents, 7, 11, 14, 25, 46–47, 49–51, 57, 59, 75
partners, 7, 31, 33–34, 42–43, 45–46, 48, 54–55, 57–58, 63–65, 67–68, 70, 75, 76–77, 80, 88, 91, 100–101

personality, 9, 24, 30
pregnancy, 45, 52, 54–55
pressure, 19, 54
privacy, 43, 51, 89
protection, 51, 54, 77
puberty, 9

red flags, 84
rejection, 42
risks, 17, 19, 43, 45, 54
romance, 6–7, 18, 30, 33–36, 42, 46, 52, 54, 57, 75, 77, 79, 88, 91, 93–94, 100
routine, 70, 88, 100–101

safety, 46, 54–55, 77
sex, 6, 18, 45–48, 51–52, 54–55
sexually transmitted infections (STIs), 45, 54
stress, 22
surprises, 6, 29, 51, 91, 93, 98, 101

tension, 64, 75
texting, 25–27, 29, 36, 67, 70–72, 75, 76, 84, 89, 93, 95
threats, 67
trauma, 45
trust, 7, 18, 54–55, 77

violence, 67, 76
virginity, 47, 51, 53
vulnerability, 43, 45

waiting, 6, 54–55, 88–89, 96
working together, 26, 47, 64–65, 87–89
worrying, 6, 55, 63

ABOUT THE
AUTHOR

ALEXIS BURLING

Alexis Burling has written dozens of articles and books for young readers on a variety of topics, ranging from current events and biographies of famous people to nutrition and fitness, careers, and money management. She is also a professional book critic with reviews of adult and young adult books, author interviews, and other publishing industry–related articles published in the *New York Times*, the *Washington Post*, the *San Francisco Chronicle*, and more. If Alexis hadn't become a writer, she would've liked to have become a psychiatrist because she finds the human mind and the way people relate to each other fascinating. She lives in Portland, Oregon, with her wonderful husband, and she wants to thank her parents for providing such an excellent model of what a healthy romantic relationship looks like.